RUNAWAY RENEGADE

ELLE THORNE

BARBED BORDERS PRESS

Thank you for reading!

To receive exclusive updates from Elle Thorne and to be the first to get your hands on the next release, please sign up for her mailing list.

Elle Thorne Newsletter

RUNAWAY RENEGADE

A wickedly sexy sci-fi new adult serial that continues... this time with a new couple and a new set of problems!

You remember Ali, right? This bad girl wasn't our favorite. Let's find out what she's been up to!

Renegade

Ali's got color-changing skin and wings. On her planet, the skin is normal, the wings--not so much. Not on females. She doesn't want the wings. And she most assuredly doesn't want the prophecy that comes with the wings. What's next?

Runaway

Ali smuggles herself to Earth. A fresh start in a fresh place, where there are no expectations, no boundaries. Or so she thinks. But she's got restrictions placed on her by her own kind, even here on Earth. What's a woman to do?

Runaway Renegade

The solution? Fit in somewhere. Where can a woman with wings and shimmering color-changing skin go? Easy! An exclusive nightclub where bodypaint and costumes are the norm.

What she didn't expect to be the norm was the sexy stranger. Thane put the S-E-X in sexy. And he's got more secrets than she does.

1

———

hane gave his best friend Zale a dirty look. *Is this summit meeting ever going to end?*

Zale responded with a slight shake of his head. Enough of a warning to let Thane know he needed to watch it, that he didn't need to catch the attention of the other Brethren.

Thane responded with the tiniest of eye rolls.

On a mountaintop in Asia, in a location that was not meant to ever be anything but anonymous, in a building that was not as old as its thousands-years-old visitors, many beings met to give their reports. The visitors to the location were known amongst their kind as the Brethren.

Thane was one such being. A thousands-years-old being, a Brethren. From nowhere near Earth.

He did not relish the cold temperatures on this

mountaintop in Asia. Nor did he enjoy the meetings. If he ever had, it was so long ago that he no longer remembered it. He missed his home in Los Angeles, he missed the warm temperatures, and he missed his human friends. He was eager to report his findings, to hear the other Brethren's reports, and then to return home.

He shivered and eyed the dainty porcelain cup of Himalayan tea that the senior Brethren's humans served. What he wouldn't give for a good espresso right now. The sooner he was finished, the sooner they'd be dismissed and allowed to return home.

Thane studied the other Brethren, tried to see them from the perspective of a human. The Brethren were Dumarian. A race from far, far away, the Dumarian sent the Brethren to Earth as guardians to protect humans from self-destruction, and from other paranormal beings.

The Brethren were handsome, every one of them, and only male. They bore a resemblance to humans with the exception of a few details. These details were not minor and had given rise to some of Earth's myths, specifically those relating to dragons.

Human heads, with human features; arms and legs like humans, though taller than most. They were all six-foot-eight. This height did not seem as extraordinary in the present time as it had centuries ago, when it awed humans who were often barely above five feet.

The Brethren's natural skin color was a darker gray. Scales merged with skin, undulating, shifting, and glowing gray and black. They had a set of magnificent wings, black as onyx, with a hook on the topside of each wing, in the center. The wings were not for show. They were fully functional.

The Brethren had been mistakenly called dragons centuries and centuries ago, giving rise to the myth of dragons on each continent. They had no fire-breathing skills. Rather, they found amusement in that claim.

What the Brethren did have was the skill to compel thought. Which is how the fire-breathing myth came to be. Long, long ago, one of the Brethren thought it would be entertaining to compel the humans into believing he could breathe fire. It couldn't be said that Brethren had no sense humor, for the fire-breathing incidents created mirth amongst the Brethren for ages.

"Thane." It was Brohm, the most senior of the Brethren on Earth, the one to whom the monastery belonged.

Thane had completely tuned everyone out. Was it his turn to speak? He nodded, waiting, unsure if there was a question on the table or if it was his turn to report.

"On the topic of Saraz," Brohm prompted. "You have news?"

Saraz, a Brethren exiled to the planet of Kormia more than a thousand years ago for violating a tenet. Saraz's violation: He procreated with a human. His indiscretion was discovered centuries later in the form of a hybrid species, long after Saraz's human mate had died. Her children had children, and so on and so forth, until finally a remote village in the mountains of the country now known as Italy had a concentrated gene pool based on the one known as Saraz. An entire isolated village of creatures, called the Asazi, a result of being segregated from new gene pool sources. This isolation had concentrated their DNA and made the mating between Brethren and human obvious.

Furious, the Brethren had banished Saraz and imposed sanctions on him and his progeny. The sanction was they never return to Earth. None of them. Not Saraz, and not his progeny. Asazi were one of two races that lived on Kormia. The other race... those were the Kormic. The Kormic history was a different sad, sad story.

Thane was put in charge of keeping an eye on Saraz, making sure he didn't return, or send his progeny to Earth in his stead. This was not a task that Thane ever wanted. He didn't agree to be a Brethren in order to become a keeper.

"Everything is in order," Thane replied.

"If you find any Asazi, you do know what to do?" Brohm asked.

Brohm asked that question of Thane so many times that by now, Thane's patience had worn thin. Why was the most senior of Brethren so worried that Thane wouldn't do his job? Because his predecessor had failed, Thane reminded himself.

Thane knew what do. He'd known since Saraz was first exiled. He wasn't charged with this responsibility when the Asazi had come to Earth. He was put in charge after Elinth had failed and been sent away.

Thane believed the entire matter was blown out of proportion. He was not fond of dealing death to innocent ones. He'd retired because he'd tired of that calling. He'd had enough of death-dealing from centuries ago, before he was made a Brethren. These were things he was not supposed to remember.

He sucked in a deep breath, and spewed his response in one quick sentence. "Eradicate them without leaving any evidence of their existence."

That answer had been memorized long ago, but never put into play because the Asazi had never returned to Earth since Elinth left and Thane took over.

Brohm and the other Brethren nodded.

How would Thane know if they came anyway? If

he met one face to face, he wouldn't know unless they were in their natural form. With their shifting ways, the Asazi were as adept at hiding in human skin as Thane's kind was. No wonder poor Elinth had never found out the Asazi had been coming to Earth to fulfill their need to incorporate humans in their breedings. Asazi looked just like humans when they shifted into human skin.

Thane wasn't going to make the same mistake Elinth had. He monitored transmissions by all the private and government agencies that observed extraterrestrial findings. He had access to their reports. He rested easy. Nothing was out of place.

Thane had another ace in the hole. The Kormic Elders kept him posted on Asazi and Saraz's activities.

Thane made a mental note to contact the Kormic Elders that provided him with updates. It occurred to him that he hadn't heard from them in a while.

Itching to return home and to his human form, having found that his human skin was far more preferable for him these days, Thane rushed through his report, giving a quick summary.

In the beginning he'd struggled with converting, preferring to have his wings and body in their more freeing saural form. Now, centuries later, he no longer felt that way. He preferred being in his human form.

The only time he couldn't control his form was

during sex. Specifically, during his climax. It was as if his entire body was so concentrated on the climax that he couldn't expend what was needed to keep his human form. His wings would unfurl, his skin would undulate, gray scales turning to glossy black, then back after the climax.

Sex with humans would have been difficult. One climax and the secret would be out.

Compelling thoughts and actions made sex possible. Compelling human females into thinking they didn't see what they thought they saw, making their memories of his transformation vanish, that was the saving grace. Without that, Thane would have been forced to live a life of celibacy.

Thane never let his sexual conquests verge on anything that would be permanent or lead to procreation. He made very sure that he did not violate tenets. He had no desire to be in the same situation as Saraz—abandoned on a planet, going crazy. Then again, Thane wondered if Saraz had been on the crazy side *before* he was banished.

"Next order of business," Brohm announced, turning to Zale.

The sooner Zale got through his report, the sooner they'd get out. Thane gave Zale a look that said "Hurry the fuck up".

2

———

*A*li's phone vibrated. She stretched, enjoying the warmth of the sun on her limbs. She unfurled her wings to let the sun caress them, and then looked at the screen. It was Antoinette. Toni, as she preferred to be called. One of her friends. She pressed on the screen to accept the call.

"Ali, we're going out tonight. You're off. You're going."

That was so typical Toni, telling people what they would do without asking. Toni's invitations were always phrased as demands. No one minded, because they always enjoyed whatever she had planned.

"Where am I going?"

"The Other Side." Toni had been talking about going to The Other Side since Ali had met her. She said it was an all-costume kind of place, body paint, exotic, anything went. "Look it up so you can see how to dress."

"What time?"

"We'll pick you up at ten."

After hanging up, Ali took a second to put The Other Side into the browser on her cell phone.

It was a club. Of course, where else would Toni be inviting her? She scrolled through the pages. There was a recurring thing she noticed in all the pictures on the site. It looked like one big a masquerade party. As if the whole club was a masquerade.

She noticed some text at the bottom. Zooming in on it, she read, "Dress code: Formal, fetish, or fantasy." She tapped through the pictures again. Fairies, animals, body paint, pirates, Vikings, French maids... looked like any costume was acceptable.

She looked down at her skin, shimmering a darker green now. She curled her wings forward, almost embracing herself, and touched her wing tips. She'd fit right in.

And she would be in her own skin.

Ali was born Alithera Grazentiva on another planet, a little more than two of Earth's decades ago.

Ali was Asazi.

A fact she was still trying fiercely to erase. She stretched, basking the late-morning sun that came through the blinds in her one-bedroom apartment in the American city of Los Angeles in a sunny state named California. This escaped Asazi had found more than refuge on Earth. In her mind, she'd found home.

To Ali's mind, the only thing she needed to fear was her own kind finding her. Particularly since she was linked to their prophecy about the savior.

In the few months she'd been on Earth, she'd learned everything she could about humans and, specifically, American society, assimilating rather well, she thought.

She embraced appearing as a human now, having left being one of the Asazi far behind, and she would never return to her planet of Kormia.

It wasn't difficult learning the American ways and languages. Asazi were taught much about Earth in preparation for what they hoped was an inevitable population migration to Earth, long ago their home planet.

Ali had the papers to work, drive, and live in America, thanks to her luck in eavesdropping on a fellow Asazi who'd come to Earth. Though he didn't know it, she'd overheard Kal talking about the contact information of people who could help her get identification papers.

They were good fake IDs, since they'd enabled her to get a job and begin a new life. There was not much that concerned Ali anymore. She felt comfortably sure that no Asazi were hunting her. She trusted Finn to keep her secret.

She studied her Asazi skin in the subdued morning light. It shimmered a pretty green color, showcasing her happiness. She'd hated her Asazi skin for so long, hated that it would change color with every emotion that passed through her, making it difficult to have a private thought or even to lie, if she were so inclined.

The wings... those were worse. Her hate for them infused her with the energy to escape her home planet and all of the Asazi. If it weren't for the cursed wings, she wouldn't have had to leave Kormia.

Asazi women didn't have wings. They weren't supposed to. Only the males had wings, and they were born with them.

Except for Ali.

The holiest of prophecies for the Asazi people was that a winged woman would be the mother of their savior.

The Asazi prayed to the god Saraz, the one behind the prophecy that the savior would be the son of a winged Asazi woman and Saraz himself.

For the first twelve years of Ali's life, all was normal. She played with her friends and was secure in her future. In typical fashion, she had an arranged marriage to an Asazi man named Finn. They were promised at the age of two.

Ali and Finn grew up as the best of friends.

Then puberty hit, and everything fell apart for Ali. When Ali went through puberty, breasts weren't the only thing that popped out. Her wings sprouted. She went to her mother, crying about the pain in her back, and let her mother look. Her mother saw the wings and cried. From that day on, her mother had bound Ali's wings, making sure they were hidden.

But still, she felt confident after she and Finn had wed and she told him her secret, Finn would keep her secret safe. She'd be able to have a normal life, children, and a loving husband. She'd never have to reveal that she was a winged freak.

That changed the day Finn told her he was breaking the Binding, and nullifying the betrothal. At first, Ali believed that she'd escaped discovery completely and could live the rest of her life as a spinster, without having to divulge her secret.

Then she heard a rumor from her cousins that her uncles were trying to arrange a new Binding for her. Since she was fatherless, and this was customary amongst the Asazi people, she couldn't refuse.

She had no interest in being a part of the prophecy of a god she didn't believe in. There was no such thing as a god, no such thing as Saraz. Ali and her mother managed to hide her wings for a decade, and would have done so longer, but an imminent arranged marriage would have ended it.

The charade would have been up the moment the groom saw her wings. He would have revealed her secret.

That's when Ali made the decision to leave; she'd just had to wait for the opportunity.

When she saw Finn's cousin Kal preparing to travel to Earth, she knew what she had to do. She broke Asazi law and left Kormia without permission. Ali stowed away on a transport bound for Earth.

She'd never regretted that decision. She regretted several things in her life, but leaving Kormia was not one of them.

She'd found employment, learning quickly that working in bars enabled her to keep a low profile, make cash, and didn't raise eyebrows when she quit and moved on. She'd worked in bars in Texas, Arizona, and New Mexico, finally settling in Los Angeles. If things didn't work out here, her next place to check out would be Las Vegas. But thus far, she'd enjoyed her stay in LA. Something about the name of the city, Los Angeles. The Angels. Angels had wings, and symbolically, it appealed to Ali. For now.

She'd assimilated to the American culture rapidly, embracing all parts of it, enjoying it fully. The only thing that was difficult to enjoy, and more so than she would have thought, was sex. She couldn't have sex without her wings unfurling. As soon as she came close to an orgasm, her ability to remain in her human form vanished. Her skin began its shimmering, her wings unfurled, glorious in their diaphanous display.

She masturbated in front of the mirror several times, just to watch her wings unfurl. She would never be able to climax with a human. The thing she could never forget when she'd come to Earth, before leaving the Asazi compound, was not to let the humans know the Asazi existed. If they found out, they'd put her deep underground in a laboratory. She believed that now, having seen countless shows on their television networks about aliens. She knew that's what she was to them. An alien. Ugh. She hated that word.

She'd never had sex or even masturbated on Kormia. Asazi had no sex drive. Not on Kormia. When she'd arrived in America, things went haywire. Her sexual desires were off the charts, but other than one sexual experience with Finn, she'd remained untouched. Ali could not afford to be discovered; not on Kormia, and not on Earth, either.

No sex meant she could have no relationships—at least not the kind that would lead to sex. So she had friendships, and if she needed sexual release, she self-satisfied.

Ali sighed, remembering her first and only experience. One she regretted. She should not have seduced Finn. He was in love with another woman, and seducing him while he was asleep left Ali feeling ashamed. She'd violated their friendship when she did that. No amount of sexual curiosity or desire justified what she'd done to him. And she had been a bitch to his woman, Marissa.

She pushed the memories away. They were easier to deal with by not thinking about them.

3

———

*T*hane would have said thank god the meeting was over, because he was tired of Asia, mountaintops, and Himalayan tea, but he didn't believe in god. Not the kind of god that humans did. He wondered if *he* would be considered a god by humans still. Centuries ago, the American natives used to think so. Humans were more sophisticated now in terms of technology, and far less believing in terms of faith.

"I'm ready to get the hell out of Burma." Thane took off the customary Brethren robes they all wore to the meetings.

"It's Myanmar, now," Zale said.

"Who cares? I don't know how many times I have to keep relearning the new names for old countries. Enough already." Thane hung the robe in the tiny closet in the room he was assigned to use every time they returned. The room was smaller than the smallest bathroom in Thane's Los Angeles penthouse apartment. "And Brohm's fixation with Himalayan tea... really? When does he want to join us in this century? Anyway, no matter what he does or thinks, none of us are going to think the way he does. I'm not interested in emulating his ways." Thane cocked a brow at Zale. "Are you?"

"Why would I be?" Zale folded his arms over his chest, his shoulders broad, his dark scales shimmering. Beneath the robe, Zale's wings moved, making waves in the fabric.

Zale was there to say goodbye. With the meeting over, all of the Brethren would be flying out, taking wing toward their respective countries. Thane was ready to leave Brohm's home behind.

"He still creeps me out." Zale kept his voice low.

Thane didn't need Zale to tell him who "he" was. Brohm. Most senior of the Brethren. "Keep your voice down," Thane advised. If Zale pissed Brohm off, who knew what repercussions Brohm would wreak on him? "I can't imagine tolerating these meetings without you. Still coming for a visit next month?"

Zale's territory was down south. Way south. Argentina. "Looking forward to it. Your grasp on the American idioms and slangs is impressive." He cast an envious glance at Thane. "I'd be open to a reassignment."

"You're just jealous because I have Los Angeles." Thane laughed, though he knew better. Zale enjoyed his retreat in Argentina. Zale didn't mind humans, but he didn't necessarily seek out their company.

"I'm out." Thane opened the window and looked out over the forested greenery below, thousands of feet to the gorge that was thickly treed.

The monastery was built into the mountain's unclimbable face, clinging to the rocky, tree-covered surface like a cat clings to a tree's bark as it scales higher, defying gravity and the odds of falling into the deep gorges below. Brohm had selected his home well. Visitors would have a hard time coming here. As would enemies. Unless they were winged, Thane noted, spreading his own hooked black wings, fully converted to his saural form.

The sun had set, dusk was on its way out, giving him the dimness he'd need to fly over the gorge and the villages, skirting mountaintops and freezing until he finally reach the hotel in Mumbai. Then he could get on a flight and head home to Los Angeles. Flying halfway around the world sucked.

HE'D JUST FLOWN IN, still in his saural form, at home in his luxurious penthouse apartment, comfortable and warm, Thane looked in the mirror, converting, his bones narrowing, his scales receding behind human epidermis. His wings folded and slid under the skin. He studied his human form.

"Handsome devil." He adjusted his tie, smiled at his reflection, then quickly sobered as the age-old questions came back to him. *Was* he a devil? Was he a demon? Was he an angel? He had no memory of ever being anything but a death-dealer, and then a Brethren.

When he'd asked Zale about it, Zale said he had no memories of home either.

All Dumarians located on Earth had been compelled to forget their pasts before being initiated as Brethren. Something went wrong with Thane, though, because he remembered being a death-dealer. He'd never shared his memories with anyone, not even Zale. When Thane asked Zale if he remembered anything from his days prior, Zale said he remembered nothing. So Thane kept his secret.

But Thane had questions, and he felt sure that Brohm had the answers, but something about Brohm made Thane suspicious. He wasn't going to go to Brohm for answers. He didn't trust him.

"Fuck it," Thane commented to his reflection.

"Fuck it." He'd become quite accustomed to the American slang and ways. Too accustomed, if he were to tell the truth. He enjoyed this time better than he'd enjoyed any other. He fit in comfortably, more than any other location in any other century.

He was meeting some of his human friends at The Other Side. With The Other Side's rigid dress code—fetish, fantasy, or formal—Thane could enter without converting and fit right in. Or he could wear a business suit, specially provided by Zale's favorite Italian tailor.

The fetish part wasn't necessarily Thane's flavor, though he did enjoy the view when the ladies paraded their attire and accessories, particularly if the attire was body paint.

It was after midnight when Thane went to the rooftop of his apartment building, converted into his saural form and took off toward The Other Side.

Cab? Who needs a cab when you have wings?

Fifteen minutes later, he alit on the rooftop of a building not far from The Other Side, converted into his human skin, and adjusted his suit with its customized slits for his wings. He took the stairs to the elevator on the fourteenth floor, then the elevator the rest of the way down. A block later, he encountered the crowd that composed the line waiting to get into The Other Side. The clubbers wore body paint, some in the forms of animals, some as painted-on lingerie. In addition to those in body paint, there were a few furries, some elves, a sexy wicked witch. Many of the men wore suits, though a few opted for Viking attire, barbarian loin cloths, and even firefighter gear.

Within moments, he was in front of The Other Side. The bouncer waved Thane in, without checking his ID and indifferent to the fact that the line outside stretched around the block. Thane was VIP. He should be; he was friends with the managers, Brad and Calder.

What neither Brad nor Calder knew: The Other Side was owned by Thane.

The club wasn't too packed, even though the law would allow more. They didn't like patrons to have to elbow each other, crush props, or rub off body paint.

Thane made his way toward Brad and Calder's reserved table. One of the waitresses saw him, waved then approached. Heather... that's what he thought her name was. Maybe. Hell, he wasn't sure, it could be Hannah. She was in body paint, and that was it. Her entire body painted a rich, vivid orange with black stripes. A set of tiger ears perched on top of her head. The staff had the option to wear any of the dress code.

The waitress leaned in and kissed him on the cheek, her paint-covered breast landing on his arm.

"Hey." Her voice was high-pitched and grating. "The usual?"

He nodded. Alcohol had no effect on his system. Some sort of immunity. It was the same for all the Brethren. It was no different than drinking water. He joined Brad and Calder. They were surrounded by the usual groupies, regular club girls looking for free drinks, bartering sex for alcohol and a good time.

4

———

Outside of The Other Side, half a block away from the front door, where bouncers almost too wide to fit through doorways were waving clubbers in. Ali, Toni, and three of Toni's friends stood in line, waiting to get in. Toni had tickets, but because they weren't labeled VIP, they didn't get in directly.

After the pictures she'd seen on the internet, Ali had opted to play it semi-safe in terms of outfits.

For tonight's venture to The Other Side, she had chosen a halter top and a miniskirt. Not ultraconservative, but far more modest than the body-painted, nude goddesses and the bikini-clad water nymphs that abounded in line. Maybe a better name for the club would have been The Wild Side.

Ali's halter top allowed her wings to protrude. With

her shimmering skin and diaphanous wings, everyone assumed she was a fairy.

She tried not to stare at the women who only wore body paint, their breasts otherwise bare, nipples evident, some hard, some not. Beneath the bright street light, Ali couldn't tell what they were using to keep their nether lips from showing because that would mean staring. She didn't want to do that.

She didn't care if they were naked, though the old Ali may have been a bit squeamish about it. On Kormia, Asazi women covered their bodies in pants or robes, unless they served in the military, in which case they wore tailored uniforms that would blend in to whatever part of the area they were assigned, be it Midland or Heartland.

"Isn't this exciting?" Toni was a couple of drinks away from slurring her words. They'd all been drinking in the car on the way over. All but Ali. So she'd driven.

It *was* exciting, in a titillating, sexy way. Though the last thing Ali needed was to be turned-on. At least if she was turned-on tonight, it would blend well with her outfit.

A thought came to Ali. She brushed it aside, but it kept returning. She could have sex in this club, in her native form, and no one would know because she'd already have her wings out and they'd assume her skin changed colors because of body paint.

Did she really want to risk discovery?

She pushed the thought aside.

Again.

ALI ROAMED around The Other Side, watching the people dance, enjoying the variety of outfits. The music was loud, with a beat that made her want to move with it. She would have been aghast at the amount of skin displayed when she'd first arrived on Earth. By now, she'd seen more than her share of X-rated videos, movies... even music videos were explicit, with dancers resembling strippers.

Who was she kidding? Certainly not herself. She'd been here two hours and she was still wide-eyed about the place, and a bit about the outfits, not because of her Asazi roots. No. Not at all. She'd thought that her time on Earth had hardened her to so much.

A girl in a body-painted corset approached a table where a man sat. He was tall, blond, tan. Ali didn't expect the girl to lean over and unbutton the man's pants, taking out his member and... The rest of Ali's view was blocked as the girl lowered her head.

Another man dressed as a gladiator, wielding a

shield, approached the bent-over girl. Moving the fabric of his costume aside, he pushed the girl's legs apart and set his shield on her back. Lining up his body, with one swift stroke, he was inside the girl, pumping in and out.

Ali averted her gaze and walked away. The club had a no-rules type of policy, it seemed. She was sexually turned-on; she couldn't help it. She was witnessing the forbidden fruit that she'd denied herself out of self-preservation. She thought of that one night with Finn and the way it had felt until he'd thrown her against the wall when he'd realized it was her. Ali's skin flushed a delicate pink with embarrassment. She kept walking.

She garnered a lot of looks, some appreciative of her costume, some curious, and several flirty—from men and women alike.

It was cute until one guy decided he would be a smartass. As she walked past him, he tugged on her wings. Her wing made a creaking, tearing sound, like when she'd had the cartilage in her ears pierced a few weeks back. Tears sprung to Ali's eyes from the intensity of the pain.

She whirled around and punched the guy in the face. "Don't do that, you... you..." She was going to use an Asazi curse word, but caught herself in time. "You Dutch bag."

His hands flew to his nose. "Damn! What the fuck? It's douche bag, you bitch." He kept his hands in place and tilted his head back. Blood seeped past his fingers. "It's not Dutch. It's douche." His voice was muffled from the injury.

"Whatever. You know what I meant." Ali didn't always pronounce things quite right. She scrambled to correct herself as others began to stare. "I said douche. I have an accent. A-hole." She stormed off, working her way through the crowd, trying to keep her injured wing from sustaining any painful jostling.

How could I have screwed up like that? If the asshole wanted to, he could have called a bouncer in. They could have called the police in and have her arrested for assault. Here she was, trying to stay under the radar and to avoid being found by her people, and she'd risked it all by losing her temper and hitting him.

She wanted to be left alone.

Ali found a corner that wasn't too overcrowded to hide and cool down. She leaned against the wall. The crease where her wing met her back burned. She touched it. Bloody.

Jerk.

5

———

Thane noticed the woman the first time she made her way around the dance floor. She carried herself far differently than the other club girls. And she seemed completely sober. She was blonde, the primary thing that made noticing her odd, because he was usually attracted to brunettes.

The second thing he noticed was her outfit. She was in a halter top and a miniskirt. That in itself wasn't so unusual—it was the rest of her costume. The skin and the wings. Her skin shimmered, reflecting the club's lighting, seeming to change color. *Coolest body paint ever.* And her wings. They were expertly done. It was as if she'd stepped off the set of a movie shoot.

His attention elevated to a more alert status when a guy seemed to zero in on her. Thane's eyes narrowed, much like a predator's, but he didn't move. The guy then made a huge mistake. He tweaked her wing, more or less like a boy would snap a girl's bra.

A smile snuck its way to Thane's face when the blonde whipped around, a complete one-eighty, and popped the ingrate on the nose.

Like a pansy, the fool grabbed his nose and proceeded to whine or curse at her.

That's when Thane decided he'd had enough. He approached them. The blonde didn't notice he was there. She whirled around and slipped past him, while Thane put his hand on the man's shoulder.

"It's time for you to go, friend." Thane looked at the man's bloody face.

"I'm not going; who the hell—"

"Sure you are." Thane concentrated on the man, holding his gaze, compelling the man's thought processes without saying a word.

"I think I'm ready to go home. I'm going to ask them to call me a cab."

"Great idea." Thane patted the man on his shoulder. "And you'll never bother her again, got it?"

"Got it." The man nodded but didn't move, staring at Thane.

"Go," Thane whispered.

The man turned and headed toward the door.

Thane looked over his head, spotting the blonde leaning against a table in the corner, an expression of pain on her face.

It would be so easy to get to know her better. A quick compelling and she'd be his.

No, he didn't want her that way. He wanted her to want him.

Why was it so different with her? Why couldn't he take the easy way?

BEFORE SHE SAW HIM, Ali felt him. More like, what she felt was his intensity. She glanced up, fought to keep the grimace of pain from her face, and looked for whatever was making a wave of sensation go through her body.

There he was. His eyes were focused on her. They burned through her. That was the intensity she felt.

The first thing she noticed was how tall he was. Or maybe that was the second, because most of all the man was striking.

Strikingly handsome. Strikingly dark. Strikingly sexy.

His eyes were the deepest of browns, possibly even black. His skin was richly tanned. Every feature was chiseled.

Ali saw many good-looking men in Los Angeles, but this man, there was something markedly magnetic about him. She didn't acknowledge him, other than to return the stare.

His hair was black, the color of the darkness on the darkest of nights in Kormia, and long enough to touch his collar. And he was in a black suit with a crisp white shirt that draped across his wide chest, emphasizing muscles that had muscles. His shoulders were broad, and his arms strained the fabric of his suit. Curious, her gaze shifted lower, but she pushed her eyes back to his face as soon as she felt the warmth flooding to her face. She knew she was turning pink with desire and embarrassment. She looked down at her arms.

Exactly as she thought, the delicate shell pink of her shame was undulating with the dusky-rose pink of her lust. *Shadows be cursed.*

She wished she could hide her desire. She looked back into his unfathomable gaze, thankful that everyone would think this was her costume, because if she were amongst her people they'd be able to read her desire instantly.

The sting in her wing turned to a gradual dull ache while she kept her eyes glued on the man. What was he doing? Most men she'd met on Earth would go talk to a woman after they'd established eye contact. But this man...

Should she talk to him? She deliberated approaching him, but something about him made her core quiver the way a piano string would hum a vibration. The sensation traveled throughout, centering on the core where she achieved her pleasure, migrating to all ends of her body, leaving behind an awareness that alarmed Ali.

She couldn't talk to this man. She wasn't sure she could even look at him anymore. The sensation was too intense, it made her too nervous.

She swiveled abruptly and turned her back on him, heading away from the pulsations—or was it emotions?—the man was creating in her.

THANE WAS MESMERIZED by the woman. He'd known a variety of females in his long life. Had been with many—he wasn't ashamed to admit—from his own kind to the two-headed witches from his planet, to the shifter types on Earth. Females never held his interest for long, and he'd never been captivated this way before.

She'd stared at him with those green eyes, a fire behind them. She hadn't turned away or been shy or embarrassed. Her interest was evident, but even more so was her strength. She wasn't interested in yielding to a man. The hunter in him wanted to rise to the occasion more than ever and meet her challenge.

Then she'd whirled away, almost as if she were dismissing him, though there was nothing dismissive in her manner. Was she avoiding him? Did she feel the same attraction and was running from it?

The urge to pursue her was primal, as was the response he felt. His pulse quickened, a fire ran through his veins, a desire to take her, control her, claim her, make her his.

Brad walked into Thane's peripheral vision then stopped in front of him, a questioning look in his eyes. "Deep in thought?" He looked in the direction Thane was looking. "She's interesting. I noticed her."

That made Thane bristle, and a part of him wanted to tell Brad not to. Not to notice her. Not to watch her. Not to want her. And definitely not to approach her. He clenched his jaw and kept those thoughts to himself.

"She's never been here before, has she?" Thane made it sound casual, though he knew she hadn't. "She'd make a great addition to the staff." He looked at Brad—then he did something he had promised himself long ago that he wouldn't do. He compelled a friend.

"I wonder if she'd like to work here. I'll be right back." Brad took off in the direction of the blonde in his haste to do Thane's bidding.

As Thane watched him go, one thing occurred to him. He didn't tell him or compel him not to make a pass at her...

6

Ali wanted to turn around to look at him. To see if he was watching her leave. To see if he still had the same expression. If he was watching another woman with the same look on his face.

She didn't. She made fists of her hands, keeping them in front of her, out of his sight in case he was watching. She fought the urge to look and won. But barely.

She'd never seen a man like him before. Sure, she saw hot men daily here. It seemed all of them flocked to Los Angeles looking for acting or modeling work.

This man, though—this dark, striking, hunter of a man—was different. He wasn't good-looking, not in the way all of the men she seemed to have met were. He was unforgettable. That summed it up.

She headed toward her friends' table.

"Whhhatt's wrrrong?" Toni intercepted her just as she arrived at the table. Her slurred words told Ali she was way past drunk. "You look…"

"I stubbed my toe." What was Ali supposed to say? Some asshole hurt my wing? Ali's mind was on that dark stranger who'd been watching her. She wanted to turn around again. Still.

"Awww." Toni made a drunken, exaggerated pout.

A tap on Ali's shoulder made her jump.

Was it him?

Could he have followed her?

Was he approaching her?

She found herself wishing it was. And then she found herself chastising herself because this whole thought process was so very unlike her. She didn't respond to men like this.

No. she didn't. She never had. Not even with Finn.

She would count to three, slowly, then turn around casually.

One.

Two.

She turned around. She couldn't make it to three. But at least her turn was a slow one, when she really wanted to spin around.

She conquered allowing her confusion to show on her face so that the man in front of her wouldn't notice.

More than that, she battled disappointment from presenting itself.

The man in front of her was attractive, sure… in an LA kind of way. He was blond, average height, average face.

The man in front of her was not *that* man.

"Hi," the man in front of her said. "I'm Brad."

"Hi, Brad." Ali forced herself to be polite and look him in the face, rather than scanning behind him to see if *that* man was still around.

"I'll get right to the point," Brad said.

I hope you do, and keep it brief. Ali smiled at him, trying to think of ways to get out of this conversation.

"We're hiring." He laughed a self-deprecating laugh. "I mean to say, I'm one of the managers here. Your costume…" He waved toward her wings, then her skin in general. "It's superb. We're always looking for attractive costumes and friendly faces here at The Other Side."

Ali cocked her head. "You're offering me a job?"

"You interested?"

Toni popped her head between them. "She shuu-uure is. You're hired, Ali."

Ali's smile was sheepish. "You'll— I'm sorry… my friend…"

"Understood." Brad reached into his pocket, pulled out a card. "I hope you're interested. My info's on the card. Stop by some afternoon before five." Brad put his hand out.

Ali shook it. "Thank you."

With that, Brad was gone, and Toni was jumping up and down like a pesky leprechaun. Which would fit, since she'd worn a green, shiny latex-looking dominatrix outfit for the night's outing.

"You got to take it. You know how much they pay here?" Another jump, then another, and another. "And now I can get in anytime, without having to stand in line or pay." Toni punctuated every other word with another leap.

Ali feared if Toni kept up the jumping, she'd puke. She put her hands on Toni's shoulders, pressing her down, keeping her feet on the ground. "Job's that good?"

"Yes!" Another one of Toni's friends, Amber, whom Ali had met for the first time tonight, butted in, envy clear on her face.

Ali remembered *that* man, his face crossing her mind. A second later, that sensation hit her again. The same sensation she had when *he* had looked at her. She raised her eyes, scanning the club, looking for his darkness, his sexiness.

There he was.

He was talking to Brad, but his eyes were focused on Ali with the intensity of a high-powered laser.

7

*D*ays Later...

Thane watched Ali telling the others goodbye as she prepared to clock out and leave. He was in his office. An office that no one else ever entered. Brad and Calder were under strict instructions not to use it, told it would only be used by the owner if he were ever in town.

There was an entrance to the office from the outside, so Thane could be in there all night and no one would see him come or go. The inside walls were two-way mirrors, so he had a view of the dance floor as well as the employee area.

Since the day Ali accepted Brad's offer, every night, Thane had sat behind the glass and watched her. Even with the glass separating them, she made his body course with electricity. He wondered if she'd experienced the sensation.

Thane had carefully avoided her. He'd like to blame his avoidance on so many things, but he knew it all boiled down to one: the dream.

Every night, she came to him in his dreams, clung to him, wanted him. He shared with her in his dreams. Shared his images of his days as a death-dealer. Shared his life as a Brethren, shared the histories of the lands he'd been in, the things he'd seen.

Every morning when he awoke, it was as if they'd been together the night before. Why had he never dreamed of her like this before he'd met her? Did she awaken something within him?

He had reservations and trepidation over their connection. He'd never felt something so deep for a member of the opposite gender, in any species. The connection was *too* deep. What was she feeling? Did she sense anything at all?

She exited through the front door. He knew where her car was parked. He'd follow her again, as he did every night after she worked. He'd fly above her car, make sure she made it to her apartment complex safely, then ensure that she walked into her place without incident. Only then could he go home and go to bed, once more to visit her in his dreams.

The change in him was drastic, and it had not gone

unnoticed by his friends. He was no longer at the club every night—or so Brad and Calder thought. They had asked him why he no longer came to The Other Side. He wished he could tell them he'd been there all along. Keeping his secrets was weighing on his soul.

He slipped out of the door to his office and into the alley, ready to convert into his saural form and follow her.

Locking the door behind him, he turned, eager to catch up.

"It is good to see you," a voice that had no business in LA said.

Brohm.

8

———

When Ali started working at The Other Side, the best perk was that if she wanted to be in her own form, she could. All she had to do was change what she wore. Be it a halter top and miniskirt, like what she wore the night she was offered a job, or a bathing suit, or even at times a glittery backless evening gown that showcased her wings and ever-shimmering skin.

Sure, she made a lot of money, but money wasn't something that she craved. She didn't covet the things that money could buy. The only thing Ali wanted more than anything else was not to be found by other Asazi. So far on Earth, she'd encountered none, thankfully.

The one thing that made her sad was that she never saw the dark, sexy stranger again. She wished she'd reached out now. If only to figure out why he made her body and mind react to him.

She'd dreamt about him, but it was such a removed dream, as if she'd been watching herself with him through another person's eyes.

She turned the key in the ignition and noticed that, for the first time since she'd started the job, she wasn't having that sensation she had every time she left work —a feeling of being watched. It wasn't unlike the night she saw the dark stranger, just not as intense as when they'd locked eyes.

9

Brohm stood ramrod straight, his body tight.

"Greetings." Thane kept his curiosity from showing.

Brohm crossed his arms. "How are you?"

Like he gave a damn how Thane was. What was his agenda? "Fine."

"Shall we go to your place?"

In the near distance, Thane could hear the knocking of Ali's engine, by now familiar to him and his extrasensory hearing.

His home was the last place Thane wanted to go with Brohm. No place at all would be his preference. He glanced toward the direction he knew Ali was driving, a longing expression fleetingly passing over his face. He caught it quickly and went stoic once more.

Thane nodded to Brohm. "We can." *Damn it.* He hoped all would go well with Ali, then cursed himself for being a silly, love-struck fool. Why would anything go wrong? It never had. She always made the early morning drive without incident.

A SHORT FLIGHT LATER, Thane was opening the door to his apartment and gesturing for Brohm to follow him in.

"To what do I owe a visit from the senior Brethren?" Thane dove into the heart of the matter. He was far from eager to have a social visit with Brohm before delving into the cause of his visit.

"How are things with The Other Side?" Brohm asked, his expression saturnine.

"That's not why you are here." Thane crossed the room opened the sliding glass door that led to the balcony, pulling sheer curtains in front of the glass. A balmy breeze blew the curtains open.

"True. It is not."

Brohm stalked in front of Thane, pacing from one end of the room to the other in a loose elliptical shape, his typical Brethren robes flowing behind him, wing slits hidden in the folds. He was an imposing figure, the way the fabric clung to the muscles he had plenty of. Thane would not like get into a scuffle with him, they were too evenly matched, with the exception of Thane's death-dealer training. Thane wondered what Brohm knew of his training, if anything. The desire to ask burned at him.

Brohm stopped pacing and faced Thane. "There has been talk. I thought I should check on it myself."

That wasn't very specific. Was this a fishing trip? Thane narrowed his eyes. "Go on."

"That Asazi have left Kormia again. And come to Earth."

"Impossible," Thane exclaimed. *Shit.* He'd forgotten to contact the Kormic Elders for a status check. *Damn it.* His mind had been so tied up with Ali. He scrambled for a response. "I'll double check on this."

"I expect a full accounting of your findings." Brohm rubbed his jaw with long fingers, his eyes full of suspicion. "By the day after tomorrow."

"Of course," Thane responded. *Will you get out of here, already?* Thane was hoping he could make a quick pass over Ali's complex, to make sure her car was in its place and she was home.

Brohm nodded, flung the curtains aside, pushed his robes off his wings, and stepped onto the oversized balcony. With a brutal sweep of his wings, he was airborne and flying into the night, away from the moon.

Thane followed Brohm onto the balcony, ascertained the senior Brethren had gone out of sight, and then made a smooth push off into the balmy breeze, banked left, and headed toward Ali's apartment.

THE ENTIRE FLIGHT to Ali's complex, Thane's mind was troubled by Brohm's visit. What had motivated him to come check on this matter? It didn't seem that it would be a large enough deal to bring Brohm from his mountainside monastery retreat. Why did he have a personal interest in seeing the Asazi kept on Kormia? Certainly Saraz's punishment was deserved, but could the Asazi really be a threat to mankind?

He shook Brohm from his mind, and decided he would contact the Kormic Elders tomorrow. He felt confident they'd tell him what they always had, that there was no cause for concern. That the Asazi were on Kormia, and Saraz was under control and living a life that made him happy with his countless concubines.

There it was—Ali's car, in its spot, just as it should be. He flew lower, closing in on her apartment. Perhaps he'd look into her window—just to make sure she was fine.

Yes, nothing creepy. Nothing stalker-ish.

Who the hell am I kidding? This is ridiculous. I'm acting like a lovesick puppy.

Odd. There was no light on in her apartment. She typically went home and read or watched TV to unwind before she went to bed.

Sick that I know her routine.

Still, odd that there was no light on. Her place was on the third floor. He set down on the landing in front of her apartment, and stared at her door. He converted into his human form quickly.

A clicking sound alerted him. The door unlocking.

The door was opening.

Too late to fly off.

Damn.

10

———

*A*li clutched the baseball bat with a white-knuckled grip. Whoever it was out there, she was ready for them. She shifted to her human form quickly, unlocked the door as quietly as she could and stood next to it. She swallowed her fear down. Was it a fellow Asazi, here to take her back to Kormia? Was it Kal? Would he turn her in if it was him?

She threw the door open with all her might and ran onto the landing, the bat cocked.

She crashed into a tall, dark form in a black suit.

"You," she hissed, which was the best she could do with the lump of fear a solid entity in her throat, blocking speech.

"Me?" the man asked, raising a brow, putting a finger on that chest of his, a wide, musclebound chest.

His voice was just like it had been in her dreams. It

coursed through her mind, striking all the right neurons, protons, and electrons, leaving behind a searing buzz that was oddly pleasurable.

His eyes were the same intensity as that night. His gaze sparking a surge of energy that flew through her body with the speed and force of a fireball.

She didn't lower the bat, though she couldn't explain why; she felt no concern at all that he was a threat to her. What she did want was an explanation for was his being there.

"Yes." She took a step back, putting distance between herself and the man who didn't seem a stranger at all. It was as if she'd always known him. "You." She pointed his way with the bat's tip. "Explain your presence on my landing."

"Not happy to see me?" He looked genuinely sad.

"No. Yes. Wait." She shook the bat at him. "Answer my question and don't..." *Don't what? I don't even know what I'm saying to him. How can he have me so tongue-tied?*

"Don't what?" His smile was the same as she'd dreamt it to be. How could her dreams have been so accurate?

"Don't change the subject. Why are you here?"

"I wanted to see you again. I've wanted to see you every night since that night." He ran long, sensuous fingers through wavy, glossy hair that was darker than midnight on a moonless night. "I *have* seen you every night since that night. In my dreams. I wanted you in the flesh."

A shiver ran through her, and she felt sure that he knew the effect he had on her. It unnerved her.

THANE COULD BARELY MAKE a coherent sentence with her, now that they were alone. *What the hell is wrong with me?*

There was one thing he knew with complete certainty. He wanted this woman, and he wanted her in ways he'd never wanted any other being in his entire life. He wanted her completely, fully, and immediately.

He reined in his desire, concerned he'd scare her away. There she was—beautiful blonde hair. Her light-colored eyes had glittered with anger and fear, but were now studying him with a calmness that unnerved him. How did this female get under his skin?

And a human.

Of all the creatures he could have fallen for or been infatuated with, the last he'd ever expected them to be was a human.

He had no wish to be another Saraz, banished to Kormia or a similar planet and live an immortal lonely life without his own kind around.

She hadn't responded to his statement that he'd wanted her in the flesh. He'd made that announcement knowing full well it could be interpreted in more ways than one. Her skin had flooded with a light pink color, softer and more delicate than the inside of the tiniest seashell or the palest pink rosebud.

He reached out, just his fingertips; he wanted to feel her skin.

She sucked in a breath and glanced down at his hand, but neither flinched nor moved. Her chest swelled as she held her breath captive, drawing his attention to the way her breasts pushed out the T-shirt, her nipples hardening beneath his gaze, making him want to touch her, to taste her.

In his pants, his cock strained for release, pressing outward; constrained by the fabric, it throbbed for her. His fingertips alit on her arm, just above her wrist. He closed his hand around her, holding gently.

She was warm. More than warm, her flesh was hot beneath his hand.

THE STRANGER'S thumb made circles on the tender flesh just above her wrist, where her pulse was sure to be a giveaway of the effect he had on her. Ali's lungs burned from holding her breath, but she couldn't release it any more than she could release herself from his eyes locked on hers.

His beautiful dusky skin was even more sensual and sexy in the night's blackness.

And she didn't even know his name.

She let her breath out with a whoosh that was not silent, but as controlled as she could make it. With a release of her breath, she uttered a question. "Who are you?"

He tilted his head to the right slightly, his obsidian-colored eyes unreadable, his expression impenetrable. "I am called Thane."

His voice flowed through her body, merged with her pulse, traveled through her system, leaving behind reactions that were a testimony to the attraction between them. The tiny core between her nether lips buzzed with an intensity that was more acute than one of her pleasure-giving toys on it. Her channel flooded with her essence, weeping moisture in her desire for the one called Thane.

Ali wanted to pull back. She wanted to analyze her reaction to this man. She wanted to blame it on hormones, or Asazi-gone-wild syndrome, what she called being away from Kormia and yielding to her sensual and base sides.

But she couldn't. She couldn't pull back from him because the force between them was magnetic.

She couldn't analyze the reaction she had to him because it was too distracting, making him the only thing she could concentrate on.

"Dreams." Her voice was husky with desire. "Tell me about the dreams."

He glanced around, surveying the landing. "Here?"

She licked her lower lip. She should be more concerned, but there was something she inherently trustworthy about him. "We can go inside."

She lowered the bat. "You haven't asked me my name."

HER VOICE WAS LOWER, huskier. He knew that she was having the same reaction as him.

She wanted him as much as he wanted her.

Of course he hadn't asked her name. Of course she would notice that and bring it up. Fool that he was. He knew her name. Knew more about her than she would probably feel comfortable with at this point. But she didn't know it.

"I was going to get to that."

She stepped aside and indicated for him to enter.

He waved her in. "Ladies first."

She preceded him, turning to look at him as she

walked. "You were not outside my apartment by acci-dent. It's not as if you were just passing by…"

"I know. I know how it looks. You have every right to be concerned."

Damn it. How could he have been so careless? Naturally she'd be suspicious of him.

All it takes is a quick compelling and she'll be over it and in your arms.

No, he would not have her on those terms. Not this woman. Not this way. He wanted her. All of her. And he wanted her to want him just as much.

"Are you afraid of me?" He crossed over the threshold.

"No. Should I be?" She looked confused for a brief second.

"No. Your outfit tonight. Spectacular. And sexy. Very sexy." His voice was husky.

Ali seized upon an explanation like a drowning man seizes a life preserver. "It's the latest in body-paint technology."

Thane cocked his head. "Can't be cheap."

She swallowed her fear away. "I have a cousin in the industry."

"It's great for working at The Other Side, isn't it?"

Alarms went off in Ali's head. She looked into his eyes. "How did you—the last time I saw you... how did you know I work there?"

A fleeting expression, one she couldn't identify because it was so brief, crossed his face. He paled briefly, and then flashed a smile that didn't quite reach his eyes. Perfect teeth behind beautiful full lips. The man probably had no problem picking up women.

"I'm affiliated with The Other Side," he said.

"Affiliated," she repeated. "That could mean an assortment of things."

"Do you like working there?"

She noted the subject change but didn't press him. She'd save that for later.

"It's interesting. The money is good. Do you go there often?"

"Fairly regularly."

A flare of jealousy bit at the thought of him being there often, and all the women that went there. Insane. She was jealous about a man whose name she hadn't even known ten minutes ago.

"Then why haven't I seen you since I started there? Since that night?" She couldn't believe she'd just told him she had noticed he hadn't been around.

His smile was sincere, tilted slightly to the right, emphasizing a shallow dimple that broke the austerity of his face. "I'm glad you noticed."

Oh, he was not allowed to get cocky. No way. "Said the guy who bothered to find out where I live and followed me to my place."

"Touché." He leaned in, closing the space between them.

Time froze, standing completely still for Ali while she was caught up in the net of his gaze. She couldn't tear her eyes from his lips and wished that they were on hers. Her tongue slipped out, nervously licking her own.

They were standing in the small hallway that led to her living room. The walls felt as if they were closing in around her. Maybe that was his presence. It left her feeling as though there was naught else in the world but the two of them, in the middle of nothingness, of space.

"What would you do if..." He took the bat from her hand—she'd forgotten she still held it—and set it on the hallway table next to them.

"If..." Ali was breathless, her voice husky.

Dropping his head slowly, his lips brushed hers with a flicker of a touch, gentler than the caress of a dandelion.

"Ali." He said her name on an exhale, as if he were passing her name to her with a breath. "Ali," he said again, inhaling her exhaled breath as if eager to merge their essences. "How did you do this?"

Ali's body leaned in, her breasts against his hard torso, her thighs pressing on his.

His hand snaked through her hair, twining in it, pulling her closer to him with a fierceness and a determination that brooked no resistance.

Ali had no resistance to offer. He'd drifted in her dreams for many nights. She'd come to know him, even if she hadn't known his name.

Her lips parted, opening up to him the very core of herself. This man awakened within her that which she'd always pushed away.

She put her hand on his abdomen, relishing the hardness of his muscles, the manliness of his form, and raked it upward, ignoring the fabric, feeling the warmth of him beneath the manmade material.

He lowered his hand over her shoulders, making tiny patterns on her skin.

When his fingertips pressed onto her back, on the human skin that covered her wings, Ali gasped. Waves of desire coursed through her.

What was happening? She'd never had a reaction like this. A sensation like the climaxes she'd given herself washed over her. She moaned.

Oh, curses. Was she going to have an orgasm from the pressure he was putting on her wings beneath her skin? Ali pushed back from him.

"What is it?" Concern flooded his face. "I'm sorry. I shouldn't have done that."

On the contrary, she wanted to say. She wanted to tell him that she needed him with a fierceness that made her body ache. That she was confused by the power of her desire for him, but the direness of being discovered was worse.

11

Thane considered Ali's face, surveying her expressions for signs that she wanted him to leave. Was she upset with him? Disgusted? He hated having to keep who he was a secret from her. He wished he could show her his saural self; wished that she'd keep his secret while still finding him attractive and appealing.

She stifled a yawn, the gesture graceful as she raised her hand to hide it. The T-shirt caressed her curves, hugging her breasts, displaying their shape in a complementary way.

"I should go. You probably need to get and get some rest."

As much as Ali wanted him to stay, she knew that his presence was too much of a temptation. She'd lose it and find herself in the middle of a sexual escapade.

She'd turned toward the door, reaching for the handle, when his hand closed over her biceps, a groan emitting from deep within him.

Thane pulled her backward, turning her body to face him. His lips claimed hers, the gentleness of earlier gone, replaced with a ferocity that matched her own need.

Ali's resolve crumbled immediately. She wrapped her arms around him, her hands winding around his neck, her fingers digging into his hair, holding him in place as his tongue swooped into her mouth, dancing with hers, taking command, not giving her a moment to hesitate. His mouth was hot, demanding, and almost predatory. His lips challenged hers to meet him with an equal measure of need, to deliver all of her passion.

Thane's hands traveled to her waist. He pulled her to him, holding her body tightly against his. The evidence of his desire, a hard length that pressed against her, consumed her thoughts. Ali wanted to reach down, to touch that part of him, to enjoy him, to please and be pleased.

She pulled back slightly. She was breathless.

"I'm sorry. I was leaving, wasn't I?" His words were a tortured whisper.

She needed him. Needed the touch. The feeling of being needed. The feeling of being wanted. This was so very different than the feeling of lust that casual strangers could deliver.

Her world was spinning, the spotlight was on them; they were in a tunnel, everything around them passing with a whoosh, and yet she was still in her hallway, still in her apartment, still in Los Angeles, still on Earth.

Ali rose on tiptoes, placed her lips against his, ran her tongue over his lower lip.

"Don't." She drew a deep breath in, drawing his exhalation in, holding it captive in her lungs the way she wished she could hold other parts of him captive.

"Stay." That one word was a whisper.

THANE PAUSED. Her word was so soft. It was a command, and it was a request. It was heaven, and it promised the worst of all discoveries. Giving himself to her meant she would know. The last thing he wanted to do was compel this woman. He made himself a promise that compelling her was not something he was going to do.

He stared at her full lips. If he stayed, he couldn't guarantee himself that he'd stop before...

Maybe he could bring her pleasure and deny his

own. That way she'd not know. That way he could prolong the inevitability of her learning who he was. Her breasts rose, swelling with each breath she took, pushing the fabric up. His cock stirred in his pants, pushing forth, wanting satisfaction. Yes, his own pleasure would be difficult to keep from reaching for.

Ali leaned against him, her fingertips searing the flesh on the back of his neck. She made small swirling patterns that teased his senses.

He lowered his hand from the small of her back, letting it cup her ass, pulling her closer against the hardness that needed to be buried deep within her, pulsing, pushing, and pumping.

He kissed her, his tongue driving deep into her mouth the way he wanted to plunge deep into her body. He tasted her lips and gave her more invitation to taste his. Ali rocked her hips, the pressure of her mound against his length.

"Shalin!" He snarled the Dumarian curse word, unaware they had slipped from his mouth until she paused, stilling her body. Her eyes flew open and looked into his.

He took her mouth once more, his other hand drifting around her waist, and up, over her rib cage, caressing the curve of her breast until he encountered her nipple, a hard nub begging for touch and taste. His thumb teased it through the material, enjoying the way it pebbled under his ministrations.

Ali's eyes closed once more, fluttering shut, while a small moan escaped her lips.

Thane ripped the fabric of her top down the center, also unsnapping the hook on the front of the lace bra. In that one gesture, he completely parted her clothing, and it opened like a robe. He slipped his hand inside. Pushing the lace of her bra out of the way, he placed his thumb on her nipple.

Ali arched, nipple pressing, getting harder and harder against his thumb. He pinched it between his fingers, rolling it. Her hips pushed forward in response.

He took a step back. One hand still on her breast, he surveyed her nudeness.

Noticing that he'd pulled away, Ali opened her eyes. She glanced down. "My top..." She fingered the shredded fabric.

"I'll buy you another. I'll buy you a dozen." He traced his finger down her nipple, over the curve of her creamy breast, then down the center of her stomach. He placed a hand on her hip, then allowed his gaze to travel to the place he wanted to taste, lick, tease, and please.

A tiny triangle of hair was the perfect accoutrement to her sex. He could smell the essence of her desire. It fueled his lust, making his body course with an electric thirst that only she could quench.

She stood before him, her eyes inviting him to delve into the depths of her garden.

He sat her on an end table, spreading her legs.

12

———

*A*li shivered as Thane ran his fingertips along her bare legs, then moved up, stroking the sensitive skin that led toward her inner thighs.

His eyes were focused on hers the entire time he touched her, as if he were gauging his effect. Surely he could sense the way he made her feel? She braced herself, hands on the level wood surface while she arched her back, pushing her sex closer to him, spreading her legs farther.

The cool air caressed her folds, making her want to feel him giving her the same caress. He ran his tongue along his lips, not knowing what it meant to her, how it looked, how much she wished to have it doing things to her. Ali gripped the table's edge tightly, trying to maintain control over her aching throb for Thane.

He blew a gust of air over her mound. She gasped.

It made her muscles tighten around nothing, making her wish they had something to tighten around. She released the table, grasped his shoulders, squeezing the muscles beneath his shirt and jacket.

Thane wrapped his hands around her ass, pulling her closer to his face and inhaling the scent of her deep into his body. She could feel his shoulders expanding as he held her scent in his lungs.

His tongue darted out, running the length of her folds, following the path of her moisture down, unit he was stopped by the table, then traveling upward, licking and sucking alternately. When he pulled her folds into his mouth and sucked on them before releasing her with a pop, she groaned and threw her head back.

She fought with her wings, fought with the climax, fought to keep from revealing her Asazi self to him. At the same time, she couldn't stop her hips from rocking into him, trying to draw his tongue deep within her. His tongue entered her channel with a quick thrust, stroking her insides, pumping in and out with a speed that had her gasping.

Legs shaking, fingers trembling as she pulled his head in closer, she bucked when he nipped at her bud, his teeth scraping the tiny bundle of nerves. With his final thrust, she grabbed his head and kept him prisoner while her wings unfurled and her body released its pent-up passion in wave after wave that pulled her under, and into a tidal pool.

It seemed as if it took forever for her to get her wings to close, and the whole time, she kept his head captive between her thighs and her hands tangled in his hair.

Sweat dripped down her forehead, over her forehead. Thane raised his head, stood and planted a kiss on top of her sweaty temple. She could smell the scent of her sex on his face. It fueled her desire further. She could spend an eternity enjoying this man. His eyes glowed with a warmth that penetrated her to the core.

THANE WRAPPED his arms around her, picked her up, and carried her to the couch. Taking a seat, he arranged her in his lap, carefully, pulling her torn dress around her so she wouldn't feel ashamed to be nude in front of him.

"You're beautiful," he whispered.

Her eyes were closing, a mystical smile on her face.

A thought occurred to him that was so out of character he pushed it away. He wanted her to move into his place with him so he could enjoy her more—daily.

What if Brohm followed me? What if he pays a visit? Was I careful enough?

Shalin, he cursed inwardly. He hadn't thought of that complication. He'd get another place, and he wouldn't tell the Brethren about it. He wouldn't have children with her. The Brethren didn't mind if they were sexual with humans or other species, as long as their blood was not diluted and new species created.

He'd figure it out.

Ali sighed in her sleep, a tiny smile making its way across her full lips. Stealing a quick kiss, he pushed her hair away from her forehead and leaned his chin on her head. How did she get to him like this? How could it be that he felt like he'd known her all his life?

He had to know more about her. He wanted to know everything. He wanted to spend every moment with her. It was as if he'd been in darkness and now found light. He'd find a new place and he'd share it with her.

The hell with rules.

13

___

Ali twirled, checking her reflection in the mirror. She pulled on the dress, adjusting it over her curves. One final touch of gloss.

A knock on the door.

Perfect timing. Had to be Thane. She was way too into him. Except she wasn't. She enjoyed how into him she was. And how into her he was.

Running to the door she yanked it open.

There he was, leaning against the door, his wide shoulders tapering to a vee, a suit barely hiding the muscles she knew he had. He was taller than most men, black hair shining in the porch light, full lips curved in a smile.

The smile vanished from his face.

She froze. "What's wrong?"

"You didn't even stop to see if it was me—or who it was."

"I knew it had to be you. Of course it did. I wasn't expecting anyone else."

Thane shook his head, took her hand. "You have to be more careful."

He stepped back, let a low whistle out from under his breath. "Stunning. You're beautiful."

Ali did a quarter spin so he could admire the dress. The way his eyes drank her in, lingering on her ass, rising to her hips, then breasts as she turned back to face him made her breath catch in her throat. She felt a tingle start between her legs, quickly turning into a current that coursed through her body, leaving her feeling as if she were on a high. Her pulse sped up with desire for him.

Thane tugged on her hand, pulling her closer, one step, two steps. His head dipped, lips swooping down, claiming hers.

The hell with the lip gloss.

Ali wrapped her arms around him, her wrists meeting behind his neck.

She didn't want to go out, she wanted to stay right here and enjoy this man, by her front door, in her home, in her bed.

A sigh escaped her, sounding more like a moan than a sigh.

"Ditto," he murmured against her lips. "I want you just as much."

A grumble interrupted them. She lowered her head, embarrassed.

"Your stomach begs to differ," Thane said with a laugh. "Didn't have lunch today?"

"I forgot to. I was so busy getting ready for tonight. The dress, the nails." Ali held her hands out, the red tips perfectly matching her dress. "See."

"I see." His words were uttered, but his eyes weren't on her crimson fingertips, not at all. They were focused on her lips.

He lowered his head once more, the tip of his tongue touched her lower lip, traced its contour before leaving it and doing the same to her upper lip. Done with its exploration of her lips, his tongue plunged into her mouth, taking hers captive the same way he'd captured her heart. He nibbled and sucked on her tongue. Her breasts swelled, nipples hardening with a need to touch him. It was as if her blood had been replaced by lava, so intense was the heat that spread throughout her body.

When he pulled back, his eyes searing hers with unconcealed desire, she held her breath. If he suggested they get inside and get naked...

What the hell am I thinking?

The second that she climaxed and those damned

wings popped out, her human lover would run for the hills.

She put her hands on his chest to steady herself. "Thane." His name was a tortured whisper on her chest. Tortured with desire and denial.

"Dinner?" His word was equally tormented.

She nodded, unable to say what she wanted to say which was: No, take me inside and fuck me properly.

THANE BARELY CONTROLLED HIMSELF. His cock was bursting with a need for her. The fire in her eyes made his desire fiercer. He wanted to take her right now. What would she think? She'd probably think he hadn't had sex in a long time. He hadn't. He didn't want anyone but her. Shalin, he wanted to be naked with this woman.

He cleared his throat, fighting to regain control of his faculties. "Ready?"

Her eyes were dilated with desire, her nostrils flared with each breath, her chest rose and fell, bringing attention to the hard peaks he wanted to draw into his mouth, to lave, lick, suck, and scrape his teeth against.

A tiny sigh, almost imperceptible escaped her parted lips. She nodded.

THANE HAD MADE reservations at Dominic's. He and Ali were right on time. They strolled away from the parking lot, his arm around her waist, heading toward his favorite seafood restaurant. He was excited to show her this place.

"You'll love it." He squeezed her closer.

"I'm sure I will." Her voice was throaty.

He knew she was still as affected as he was, their desire barely kept at bay. How long could it last? Being so close to each other every day almost. How long before the damn burst and they were naked, sweaty, and he was scaring the shit out of her with his big black wings and scaly dark skin.

A shadowy figure caught his eye. *What the hell?* He froze.

"What is it?" Ali' scoured his face, as if trying to figure out what was wrong.

"I thought I saw something." *I know I saw something. The question is, what the hell was it?* It moved fast —superhuman fast—way faster than a human would.

Whatever it was, it was gone. Was it a coincidence? A supernatural being—had it followed them? Was it one of Brohm's? Was it something else? What else could it be?

"What did you think you saw?"

"Nothing, I guess. Let's go inside." He forced a smile to his face. "We better feed you before your tummy complains again."

Ali gave him a look, rose on her toes and planted a kiss on his jaw.

THE HOSTESS SAT them at a table near the window with a view of the water and the pier. The moon's crescent was reflected in the dark water.

The waitress in a black skirt and a high-necked white shirt offered to give them a few moments, asked about drinks. "Wine perhaps?"

Thane raised a brow.

Not a chance, unless you want to see me convert into a winged shimmering fairy-like creature. Ali shook her head. "No, no. Thank you. Water without ice is fine." She hadn't even become accustomed to ice, after all this time on Earth. It wasn't something she had growing up on Kormia and it felt odd, drinking ice-cold beverages. "You can have a drink. I'll drive," she told Thane.

"No. Iced tea's fine for now."

ALI PICKED AT HER FOOD. There wasn't anything wrong with it. It was excellent, actually. It wasn't the food. It was Thane. He was fine when they left the apartment, but sometime after they parked the car, he became serious—concerned. Okay, it was more than just Thane. It was her. Them. They couldn't even have sex. She ground her teeth in frustration.

"You don't like it?" He frown, his brows dipping, his tan face concerned.

"It's great."

"You're not eating much."

She managed to get through the rest of her meal, ignoring the thrumming that her body was going through every time she met his eyes. She couldn't even concentrate on their conversation, so strong was her desire for him.

No sooner did she put the fork down, than the waitress and a busser swarmed on their table.

"Something sweet? A little dessert?" Her eyes lingered on Thane.

Ali frowned. Was she really making a pass at him in front of her?

Thane ignored the waitress. "Ali? Dessert?"

Bonus points for him for not giving the waitress any attention. "Why not?" Ali gave the waitress a fake smile. "Surprise us."

"Please bring a couple of lattes, too." Thane requested.

Ten minutes later, the svelte redhead brought out two plates. Identical. A heavenly concoction of ice cream, whipped cream, mousse, and chocolate.

With a quick turn of her hip and more swaying than was necessary, she was gone.

"Looks good." Ali dipped the spoon into the dessert and put the chocolate mousse creation in her mouth. She had swallowed the first bite and wrapped her mouth around the spoon with the second one when it hit her.

"Oh, no. This has..." *Scars. The dessert has alcohol in it.* Her skin felt hot, she glanced at her arms in the candlelight's dimness. They were a tint of pink, and turning a slight orange hue.

Orange.

The color Asazi turned when angry. And she was angry. The waitress should have warned her this had alcohol in it. Ali had to get away before he she lost full control. She felt her wings tingling beneath the human skin.

No.

"Excuse me. Restroom. Emergency." She bolted out of her chair and ran to the restroom. Thankfully she'd noted where it was as they were led to the table.

Slapping the door open with her palms, Ali made it

into the first available stall without being noticed. She took her mirror out of her purse.

Her face became a blazing orange color. Behind her she could see her wings. She leaned against the door, breathing deeply. What the hell was in there? Odorless? Tasteless?

She bit back a growl of frustration. She shouldn't be angry at the waitress. She should have asked her if there was alcohol in there.

Should have.

THANE STARED AFTER ALI. Who was he to question what a woman deemed was an emergency. One moment she was fine and enjoying the dessert, the next she was gone, in a flash, heading for the restaurant. Did something in it make her sick?

The waitress stopped by. "How's dessert?"

"Fine." He frowned. Wondered if he should ask if there were nuts or something in it that would have given Ali an allergic reaction. He didn't even know what she was allergic to. Not only would he sound ignorant, but he wasn't even sure if that's what it was.

"Thanks for asking." He took a drink of his latte and pushed the dessert away. He'd enjoy it with Ali when she returned.

Fifteen minutes later, the latte was gone and so was Ali.

Still.

Pushing his chair back, he glanced out the window.

Then did a double take. Behind a post on the pier. He scrutinized the spot. Yes. There it was.

A set of glowing eyes, in the darkness. Behind the eyes, a menacing face, barely discernible in its shape. A supernatural. The same one from earlier. But not one he recognized.

Why was it following him?

The first thing that came to his mind was Ali. She had been gone too long and now this creature was outside. And he knew that just like him, other creatures could morph into a human shape. Damn it all.

"Check, please," Thane barked at the waitress, handing her a credit card. "Where's the restroom?"

She pointed.

He headed toward the restroom door, just as he reached out to shove the door, it opened. He almost fell into Ali.

He breathed a sigh of relief.

"Hi." Ali's voice was strained.

"You okay?" He looked up and down her body and face. She seemed fine, a little shook up perhaps, but then again, that could be from his scaring her by being in front of the door.

"Yes. What are you doing? Are you okay?"

"You were gone so long..." He took her hand. "I guess I hoped you were okay."

"I had a little... reaction... to the dessert."

"I wondered if that was it." He glanced behind him to see if the creature had come in. Right. Now he'd lost it. As if the creature would come in, looking like that. It would morph, and he wouldn't be able to discern that it was a supernatural.

"Ready to go?"

ALI EXHALED and glanced back at their table. The busser was already clearing it. Guess he was ready to go.

That was close.

It would be a shame to waste the beautiful night and the view of the water. "How about a nice walk on the pier?"

He frowned. "No. I don't think that's a good idea."

"Why not?"

He paused for so long she almost asked again.

"The help said that the area has had a rash of muggings. How about we go for a drive?"

A drive? She didn't want to let her disappointment show. How was she supposed to show off her pretty dress and enjoy visiting with him if they were on a drive?

"I know the perfect spot to take you for a walk. It's much safer than this," Thane wrapped his hand in her hair, pulling it lightly to tip her face up. "Up the coast a little."

He kissed her, his mouth warm, the flavor of chocolate and coffee beans were enticing.

IT WAS DAWN. Thane hadn't seen any other creatures, and he'd driven far enough and fast enough, he hoped, to keep from being followed. Their walk had been much better in an isolated park where no creatures could disguise themselves as humans and get the jump on him. He pulled up to Ali's apartment and walked her up to her front door.

"Coming in?" The invitation in her voice made his cock jump with hope.

Down, boy. "I have to get some work done." He had to find a better place for her to live. Somewhere with security. If she'd let him help. He wondered if there were a group of supernatural beings he could hire on the down low to keep her safe.

A group that wouldn't reveal themselves to her, but could be completely loyal and trustworthy. First order of business, new place. One where neither of them could be easily followed.

"Maybe I'll see you at The Other Side tonight?" Her voice was hopeful.

He hadn't been big on going, not openly. The note in her voice made him feel guilty. "Perhaps."

14

———

*I*n the break room at The Other Side, preparing for another night's shift, Ali adjusted the strap on her bikini-type top. She stepped out of the break room and into the loudness that was The Other Side.

Pausing to pick up her tray of Jell-O shots, Ali whirled when she felt fingertips adjusting the ties of her bikini top, near the base of her wings.

She laughed nervously. "You scared me."

Heather smiled a smile that didn't quite reach her eyes. "New outfit?" Heather took a step back and appraised her. "Is that for Brad's sake? Or are you aiming for Thane?"

Ali cocked her head and studied Heather's face, then her eyes traveled down the length of Heather's body-painted, busty figure. Why would she be asking about Thane? Did Heather have designs on him?

"What do you mean?"

Heather stepped closer, the tall beauty's breasts almost in Ali's face. "Don't pretend you don't know what I'm talking about." She aimed one French-manicured fingernail at Ali's nose. Her nostrils flared.

Now she wasn't sure she wanted Thane to come up here. The last thing she needed was trouble at work. If this escalated, if Heather turned it into something physical, then the off-duty cop that doubled as a bouncer might arrest Ali.

She sighed. Once more, she had to make sure she stayed off the radar. Ali clenched her hands into fists. She'd love to get physical with Heather.

"I have to get to work." Ali unclenched her hands and walked away, back stiff.

STRIDING toward the entrance to The Other Side, Thane straightened his jacket. Ali would be happy to see him. Tonight would be a pleasant surprise. He touched the delicate petals of the rose he'd picked up for her. Ivory with the palest pink tint. It reminded him of her.

The newest bouncer, Tico—wide as a table and

taller than the doorframe—stood outside. Like the rest, this one had no idea that Thane was his employer. He only knew what Brad had told him: Thane was VIP.

"Evening, Thane." Tico waved him in to the dismay, boos, and hisses of those waiting in the line. The club was already full.

He felt Ali's energy before he saw her. What was it between them that made this tangible force field? He paused, allowing the effect to sink in, relishing it the same way he relished every moment with her.

Ali stopped walking, turned, her eyes surveying the crowd, searching.

Clearly she'd felt their connection, too. She touched her hair, tucking it, twirling it, the way she did when she was nervous.

What was bothering her?

Her eyes landed on his face, locked on his. A look of consternation passed over her features then vanished, only to be replaced by a smile that was tinged with relief.

She took a step toward him then looked around. Thane covered the distance between them quickly and easily; the crowd wasn't an obstacle.

He leaned in, reining in his desire to gather her into his arms and claim her mouth with a powerful, hungry kiss.

He put his hand on her hip—bare, hot to the touch of his fingertips.

"I wanted to visit." His lips brushed hers.

She pulled back, looking around.

"What's wrong?" He frowned but kept his hand on her hip.

"I'm working—"

"I know your boss. You'll be fine." He attempted some levity. She knew he was friends with Brad and Calder. A kiss wouldn't be a problem.

Her eyes grew soft for a moment, and the look of fear subsided. Her full, lush lips parted. He groaned inwardly, wanting to take that as an invitation to kiss her.

"Thane!" A voice broke the spell, tearing him from the place he wanted to be.

Trepidation crossed over Ali's face.

Thane looked up to see who the source was. Heather.

He gritted his teeth at the interruption and smiled tersely. "Evening."

He turned back to Ali. "I have something for you."

"Where have you been?" Heather was insistent.

He looked back up, ready to throttle her. "Away."

She pouted and it wasn't a look that worked on her.

"Excuse me." He pointedly turned ninety degrees from her so she could take the hint, and looked at Ali.

Ali's mouth was an O of surprise.

"Can we have a private moment?"

ALI CRINGED, knowing Heather heard him.

"I... Well... I'm... I have to work."

"It's fine. You get a break, and we're taking it right now." His large hand took hers, warm and secure, his grip firm. He tugged on her, pulling her toward the break room.

Ali could feel Heather's agitation as the woman seethed. She didn't look up to see how angry she was. She knew she'd face that later.

Thane closed the door behind them, then he turned the lock, securing them in the room, completely alone.

He held out a rose. One single, beautiful white rose, not completely fully bloomed yet, with traces of delicate shell-pink tint. It reminded her of her own skin when she blushed.

"It's beautiful," she whispered, unsure why she was whispering when they were alone.

He tilted her chin up, and the only place her eyes could land was on his.

"Want to tell me what that was all about?"

She shrugged. "I'm not sure what you mean."

He narrowed his eyes.

She took a deep breath.

"Listen, Ali. I have never, as long as I have been alive—I have never, ever felt for a woman the way I feel for you."

She blew out a breath. Pushing her hair out of her face, she twirled a lock until he put his hand over hers, stopping the motion.

She fought back the tears that threatened. Damn the curses and shadows. She was never prone to tears. She did not cry. Her heart ached with the feelings she felt for this man. A man who couldn't walk into the same room she was in without making her body's chemistry react to his. He'd never be able to sneak up on her. She could feel him; she could feel the very essence of him.

"I believe you." She did.

"Then there is nothing to concern yourself with when it comes to Heather. I'll talk to Brad."

"No!" She didn't need any drama or any attention. "I'll take care of it." Somehow she'd find a way.

"I want you." His voice was sex-husky, his breath a warm and exotic cinnamon-clove blend.

Her body responded to his proclamation, to the scent of him, the man of him, the musk of his desire making her own flare. She felt dizzy as her senses reeled from his presence and the promise of him.

"Thane." His name was ripped from the depth of her needs, a passionate, low declaration that expressed how badly she wanted him and had wanted him since... since the very night when...

Heat rose throughout her body, flooding her being with a warmth that begged for him.

"I have to taste you. I need to be between your sweet thighs, with my tongue testing the heat of your core, pushing you to new limits."

She moaned, for she couldn't talk. Words couldn't express the passion coursing through her body, but if they could express it, her mouth was powerless. Her entire being was focused on the laser beam of his lust.

"I—" Ali began, but was immediately cut off by his kiss. His mouth pounced on hers with the ferocity of a jungle cat's, hard, demanding, not accepting anything less than all of her.

He pulled her close, his arms rigid bands of steel that brooked no argument from her body, though she had no argument to offer. The hardness of his shaft pressed against her, reminding her of that which she lived without. That which she suffered without. She knew what sex was. She knew what desire was. What Thane offered was neither sex nor desire. It was something more powerful, more giving, more taking than any type of sex or desire she'd ever imagined.

The heat of his mouth, the forcefulness of his

tongue, the deliciousness of his scent and taste were too much. When his hands encircled her waist, weeks of pent-up frustration at not being able to have him gave in a flood. The flood of moisture traveled from deep within, dropping into her channel while her longing for him coursed through her body, leaving behind jolts of electricity and surges of power. Her clit buzzed with lust, her breasts swelled, her nipples hardened, pressing against the bikini fabric.

"You're mine."

"Yes." Her moan was the verbal acquiescence to the one her body had already given.

Thane turned her around, faced her toward the wall, pressed her against it, trapped between the hardness of the wall and the steely strength of his body, punctuated by his rigid shaft, demanding access to her body, not accepting anything less.

A swift yank and he'd released her bikini top. Big, hot hands cupped her breasts. He rolled her nipples between his fingers, tugging, pulling, twisting, making her arch her back, making her ass press against his hardness.

She wiggled against him slowly, rotating her hips, enjoying the feel of his cock as it buried between her cheeks and tried to slip between.

Her legs were spreading, wanting him deep within.

He reached between them. She heard a zipper and

a rustle, then she felt the fabric of her bikini bottom being pushed aside.

His cock, hot to the touch, seared her ass as it lay on one cheek.

He groaned in response, spreading her legs wider.

The cool breeze hit her pussy, making her clench for a brief second, then the heat of his cock was pressed against her lips, couched in between her thighs, but not in her. She moved, backward and forward, letting her wet lips caress his shaft, the teasing causing her to get wetter, the moisture dripping down the inside of her thigh.

He kneaded her breast, rolled her nipple, tugged on it, almost to a deliciously painful twist.

He spread her more, baring her swollen lips as he slid his cock against her equally swollen and hard clit.

Ali lifted her hips, needing him to fulfill the promise and deliver that which she craved.

She panted, wanting to buck against him, to force him deep within her channel, to suck him in with her muscles and keep him prisoner, enveloped deep within her pussy. A moan escaped her as her eyes closed. The pressure of his cock, slightly touching her clit, tucked between her lips, going back and forth was too much. Oh, cursesofshadowsfiresofhell... she could barely breathe from desire for him.

"Please." The word was ripped from her chest, distorted by her want.

He slid a finger inside, deep, then out, slowly. Joined it with another, her muscles clenched around him. She pressed on the wall, pushing herself back onto his fingers, grinding her pussy against him.

The sensation was overwhelming. The sexual tension of being around him for so many days without so much as one climax pushed her into a place where her world shattered into a million glittery pieces and a wave jerked her under, making her gasp for breath as her body spasmed through her climax.

"So hot and wet for me." Thane groaned. The wide head of his cock traveled between her lips, touching her clit.

He pressed the thick head of his cock against her entrance and held her hips to still her movement. She moaned her frustration, trying to grind on him.

Grasping her firmly, his cock parted her folds and glided in, stretching her channel, enveloped within her tightness, piercing her pussy.

He filled her, and then pulled back, watching his thickness as it came out of her, glistening with her juices, her pink and red velvet open for him. Waiting for him to take her.

"You're so beautiful. Made just for me."

Her wings fluttered slightly as he pushed back in. Shalin, he best be careful. He knew how much she valued them. He wanted to lean forward and kiss the tender wings, but he knew she was peculiar about them, though to him they were an extension of her, even if they weren't her.

"You're mine. I'll never let you go."

"I never want you to." Her voice was a choked cry blended with a whimper.

He released his grip; she rocked back, raising her hips, arching her back, impaling herself on his thickness.

Her sigh pushed him, made him harder, the pain of it exquisite. The nights spent with her, just talking, just hugging, just kissing, had lifted him to a heightened level of passion. He grunted to keep from releasing, wanting to extend this moment forever.

ALI ROCKED ON HIM, enjoying the hard, hot flesh.

"I need you."

His breath caressed the tendrils of hair by her ear. She wasn't sure she heard him at first, thinking that she'd only imagined it, then she felt his lips kissing her right behind her ear.

Grasping her hips, he thrust into her, deep. A shock of pleasure spiked throughout her body, starting between her legs, traveling to her mind like a bolt of lightning.

In and out he pumped, driving deep, pulling almost all the way out, plunging deep once more. He filled her, over and over, filling and emptying, then filling again, over and over.

Her hips rolled then rocked, grinding and pushing. "I... this I..."

He released her hip, trailing his fingertips over her lower abdomen until he found her pulsing clit. He made fast circles with hard fingers. "Come, baby."

Ali tensed, her body responding to his command, to his request. The sound of his voice, the need in his tone, began to throw her over the edge. She lost herself fully in the sensations washing over her. Her mind felt as if each thought was shattering into tiny little fragments of fireworks while her body surged through a tornadic field.

Grabbing for something, anything, she couldn't find purchase. There was nothing to hold on to. Shoving against the wall, she pushed herself even harder against him, driving her ass into his body as her channel filled with him. An explosion pushed her over the edge. A partial scream slipped out.

"I'm coming. Damn." His words were a hiss.

His equally explosive eruption shot into her. Hot essence pulsing against her pussy walls.

Thane groaned, gripping her tight, holding her against him while his body shuddered against her back.

15

———

Thane stepped into the alley behind The Other Side. He'd left Ali to work. She'd insisted she had to get back. He breathed a sigh of relief she hadn't seen his wings.

He'd held her still, not allowing her to move or look back for fear that she'd see. He should have been far more careful. Next time—

There could *be* no next time. He cursed at his foolishness for giving in to the desire to be with her. It could have blown his identity. Then what? Then she'd have fled. It was one thing for her to wear those pretty little costume wings. It was a whole other matter for him to display his real ones. A complete other matter. She'd have freaked out and run from the room screaming, he'd have bet.

Thane wasn't paying attention. He was so wrapped

up in his thoughts that he didn't notice something was off until his senses went on alert. He whirled around, making a quick one-eighty.

A being stood before him, studying him with a dark glare.

"Death-dealer," the creature said, arching a brow, gray skin over black and red eyes. Long fingers plucked at the creature's overcoat, betraying a nervousness. The kind of nervousness that would lead to impulsive action.

"How do you know me?" Thane asked the creature, as it was unfamiliar to him, including the species. "What are you?"

"You killed my brother. Do not pretend you do not know what I am, death-dealer."

Thane wished he could remember. Walking around without knowing if he had an enemy was uncomfortable.

"What is it that you want from me?" He braced himself, ready for an attack.

"Retri—"

Sounds of loud laughter came from around the corner, interrupting the being. Humans were coming.

Reaching out with a supernatural speed, Thane wrapped his fingers around the being's bony wrist.

"You'll not seek retribution. You'll go in peace or regret it."

The being drew a blade from the folds of its overcoat. It struck at Thane, the deadly blade a wicked glint in the lamplight.

"I will—"

Thane struck quickly with lethal force. A sideways slap at the blade, calculated to avoid touching the razor-sharp edge, and the blade was airborne.

Thane snatched it midair, flipped it in his hand and, with one swipe, slit the creature's throat.

The being collapsed, its overcoat empty, now a vacant shell.

Thane held the empty coat up.

16

*W*eeks later

It was afternoon when Ali woke up. She was on her couch and Thane was long gone. She didn't know what time he'd left.

They'd been doing this for three weeks. Every night, he met her after work, on her landing. He'd bring a latte, and they'd walk to the park nearby and sit all night, talking, and on occasion kissing.

He hadn't tried to get into her panties again, and as much as she wanted him, she didn't push the issue. There was too much at stake.

She showered and changed for work, wondering if he'd be at the club, and though she wouldn't admit it, she was eager to see him and hoped he'd be there.

THANE WAS A NO SHOW.

Ali tried to contain her disappointment, but she'd had taken extra care with her wardrobe. She wanted to be the sexiest-looking fairy at The Other Side. She'd gone out and bought a new miniskirt and a new backless top with straps that crisscrossed her back, between her wings. When she'd looked in the mirror that night, she thought she looked particularly fetching.

Too bad though, because the entire night had passed without incident. And without Thane. Not a single sighting. Nothing.

Irritated, at the end of the evening she'd driven off in a huff, pulled into her apartment complex and stomped her way up the stairs to her place, refraining from slamming the door because she didn't want to disturb the neighbors.

She sat on the couch, too dejected to bother peeling her new clothing off and change into something more comfortable. She wanted to not care that he hadn't come, but she did care, and she was pissed.

A soft knock on the door made her jump, and then a surge of joy erupted in her. Who else, of course.

She opened the door without bothering with the peephole.

There he stood, calm, collected, self-assured and unreadable, in another expensive suit. Yet, so different from the man who'd held her as she'd fallen asleep last night. Remote. Almost sinister. Not her Thane. He seemed... off.

Except he was here. That's what counted.

"You're late." She wished she could bite back that response.

"I came as quick as I could." He stepped into her place, closing the door behind him, for all intents seeming to completely belong there. "I had business to take care of."

"More important than me?" She allowed a mock pout to form on her lips.

"Nothing is more important than you." He reached for her top, took the hem of it between two fingers and pulled gently, tugging her closer. "This *was* about you. Everything is about you."

She wanted to ask him what that meant and how that could possibly be, but it was difficult to talk when his lips were locked on hers, taking control of her tongue, stroking it with his, doing that eternal dance of tongues, sealing her words behind a vault of emotions and desire.

"I missed you." He breathed the words into her mouth, his hands wrapped in her hair, pulling her head back. "I thought of you all day."

"I like the sound of that." She tugged on his lapels, wrapping her fists around the expensive fabric and holding him close, her hands trapped between them. "I thought..." She gulped her insecurity away.

"Don't think. There's no room for thoughts between us, only whatever it is that's driving this forward."

"It's scary." Her voice was tiny, breathless.

"It's magnificent," he murmured against her jawline, his lips traveling down, kissing her neck, his tongue blazing a trail.

"What if—"

His lips took away her protest, his tongue taking control. A long, breathless kiss later, he held her in his embrace. "I want to know more about Ali."

"What about you?" She traced the collar of his suit, her hand wandering over the fabric, her fingers playing with his buttonholes.

"I'm boring."

"I'd rather kiss you than talk about me."

***

After a marathon of kissing Ali on the couch in the small dingy apartment, Thane wished they'd been at his place. They would have been more comfortable there, where they could have enjoyed the evening on his balcony, but he knew Ali's budget didn't allow for a nice place. And he couldn't take her to his. He couldn't risk another unexpected visit from Brohm.

Thane tugged on her top. Pulling at it, making it

clear he wanted it off her body. Wanted her naked. His cock was about to burst from kissing and touching through clothing. Pulling her up, he lifted her onto his lap so she could see what she did to him.

Then she did the strangest thing. She avoided looking at his pants, and kept her eyes on his face. She jumped up from the couch.

Ali tossed some throw pillows on the floor next to the couch.

Was this her way of saying no? He couldn't believe it after the way her tongue had danced with his and her moans had been low spurts of aphrodisiacs that drove him crazy.

Thane rose from the couch, confused, and opened the window, letting the moonlight shine in on them. He flicked the lights off. She sat cross-legged on the floor, her hands in her chin, elbows perched on knees.

He could spend an eternity looking at this woman, learning what was in her mind, what made her tick. What was so special about her that drew him to her?

He didn't want to tell her he'd spent the whole day looking into a place for them. A place where they could meet and spend time alone. A place unknown to the Brethren.

17

---

*A*li had divulged nothing of herself, or her Asazi roots, to Thane. By the same token, she'd learned nothing about him either. She wanted to know where this dark man had grown up, who his family was, where he was from.

Should any of that matter? It shouldn't. She couldn't have sex with him unless they were at the club or she was in her own skin. She shouldn't even be allowing them to spend this time together, getting attached. She sighed. Too late. Way too late to avoid getting attached.

She'd had to push him away. She felt horrible, in more than one way. Horrible because she didn't want to rebuff him. Horrible because her desire for him kept growing. And growing. And she could do *nothing* about it.

Raising her hand to push her hair back, she noted the indigo color of her skin, reflecting her sadness. She moved to the restroom, studying her skin in the mirror. Behind Ali, her wings unfurled, fluttering slightly, also a deep-blue color, though diaphanous.

Cursed Asazi wings. They were the cause of her inability to be normal. They were to blame for everything.

She stalked around her apartment, going from one room to another, furious at her predicament, hating her people, hating herself, hating everything Asazi.

She turned abruptly, continuing her pacing, back and forth in tight circles, from the kitchen to the restroom to the living area. Each time she passed the restroom mirror, her wings and skin mocked her dilemma.

With the next abrupt turn, the bottom of her wing swung wide and knocked a wooden knife block off the kitchen counter. Knives scattered, clanging as they struck each other and bounced off the linoleum, some of them leaving scars on the floor.

Ali swooped down to pick them up, catching them in her hands. One knife sliced her thumb. Blood began to drip down her hand, over her wrist and forearm to her elbow, then plopped to the floor.

She looked at the sharp butcher knife. Large and lethal.

She'd had enough of these damned wings. They'd' ruined her life on Kormia, and now they were doing the same on Earth.

Ali stormed into the bathroom. Hoisting herself up to the counter, she sat, her feet in the sink, her body angled so she could see her wings.

Taking the knife, she wrapped her arm around herself and plunged it into the base of her wings, at the lowest crease in the middle of her back.

hane took wing to the north, finding a mountain that was isolated. He alit on a dirt road that led to an abandoned cabin. This spot had long been the place he traveled to in order to create a portal that led to Kormia.

He could do it elsewhere, like in the city, but he always stood the chance that someone would see the portal. Or even worse, that someone on the other side —in Kormia—would seek to travel to Earth. That was not permitted. Not only was it not permitted, it could create complete chaos and piss off the Brethren. Here, on this isolated mountain, if anyone did decide to come over, he could pursue avenues to convince them by word or deed to go back to Kormia. Luckily, he'd never had anyone try to come to Earth.

He crossed his arms, closed his eyes and concentrated. A moment later the force of the portal's energy pulled at his being. He opened his eyes. He'd created the portal to Kormia, a shimmering mirage that looked more like the heat that rose off of a hot road than a doorway. He couldn't cross through it. No Brethren could enter their own portal. But he could wait for the Kormic Elders. It never was a long wait. They'd always sensed his portals before long and arrived.

True to this, within thirty minutes, several scarlet-robed figures appeared. Their hoods covered their faces, but he knew it was the Kormic Elders. The ones who kept track of Saraz and all pertinent events on Kormia.

In unison, they stood shoulder-to-shoulder facing him, raised their hands and pushed back the hoods. Their eyes, all white, as if they had cataracts, used to spook him and send chills all over his body.

As many times as he'd seen these beings over the span of time, he had never become accustomed to their exotic look. Though at least now, they didn't repel him as they had in the beginning, with their half-human, half-alien features. He could think of no word that suited them better than alien.

The lower half of their faces were human, with human jaws, but they had pale, raised striations that traveled from their bottom lips and converged to a point in the middle of their chins, exactly where a cleft would be, if they'd had one.

The part that garnered the most attention was above their eyes. A brow ridge that was composed of lizard-like skin traveled upward to a forehead that had two bony vertical ridges, stopping where a hairline would be. Instead of hair, the Kormic had purple-and-orange-tipped spikes.

He found himself holding his breath, as he always did when they were in front of him. They were able to walk through the portal. That would not be a good thing, and Thane was glad they didn't. He'd never tested their skills, and he was unsure if he was a match for them, death-dealing expertise or not.

"Brethren Thane." Their voice was a collective, as though they were of one mind.

He knew they could communicate silently.

"Elders." Thane nodded respectfully. He'd come to have a high regard for these beings.

"We have been trying to reach you for a long time now. Why have you been blocking our attempts?"

Thane frowned. "Blocking? I wouldn't do that." Worry washed over him. "Why? Why were you trying to reach me?"

"Asazi have made a home on Earth. In the last few months, a human traveled to Kormia then returned to

Earth. With a hybrid Asazi and human child. And her Asazi mate."

Thane's hands clenched into fists. "What the—"

The Elder raised his hand—Thane didn't even know his name. Did they have individual names?—then he continued, "And the one that Saraz seeks to fulfill his prophecy has left for Earth. An Asazi Elite, one of their best soldiers, has gone rogue and is seeking to find her to return to Saraz in exchange for his father's life. Saraz is holding this Asazi's father captive."

Thane released his fists, flexed his fingers. "How has Saraz managed to get humans to Earth again without you noticing? That's what the Elder group was created for: to prevent these exact incidents."

"Saraz is very adept at subterfuge."

"This cannot be happening." He cursed inwardly.

"We will be taking care of Saraz ourselves. The Brethren do not seem to have the Kormics' best interests in their minds."

Thane didn't want to tell them that none of the Brethren cared about the Kormic or the Asazi. They only cared about punishing Saraz by keeping him on Kormia and containing his mistakes. It wasn't such a bad idea, their handling the issue. He couldn't sanction it, of course, but he would do nothing to prevent it.

"I do not want to hear of this." That was the best he could do as far as permission went. It had to be tacit.

The Elders looked at each other, then looked at him. They nodded and pulled their hoods over their head, drawing them low until their faces and white eyes were well hidden.

A one-eighty, and with that they walked away, leaving Thane to wonder if they'd just solved his problem on Kormia and the next time he talked to them, they'd tell him the deed was done. That Saraz was no more. Now he had to figure out about the Asazi on Earth.

Thane had never been close to Saraz, but he wished him no ill. He wondered if the madness he suspected had overtaken Saraz's mind was there before the banishment or if being banished had made him insane.

None of it mattered to him anymore, it never really had—much. He was not one of those who felt as though Saraz should have been banished. Thane understood the tenets and didn't agree with what Saraz did, creating a whole new race—but the truth was, there were so many paranormal beings on Earth and in the entire galaxy, anyway. It didn't seem to be such a big deal that Saraz had added another one.

Thane watched the Elders' departing backs. Let

them take care of Saraz. He had more important things on his mind.

Like the Asazi on Earth.

And Ali.

He hadn't talked to her today.

THANE PUSHED his hair out of his face and ran through the day's events. He was still taken aback by the Elders' revelations. He would reach out to his contacts and have someone find the Asazi and take care of this. He didn't want to leave Ali, not after Heather's threat.

Would Brohm be coming to Thane for answers tonight? Probably, since this was the deadline. If so, Thane couldn't afford to be with Ali. He didn't want her to be in Brohm's sights.

The Brethren would definitely frown on his having feelings for a human female. Thane wasn't sure he could hide those feelings.

He'd stay away. He'd text her and tell her that he was out delayed at a meeting.

After Brohm visited him tonight, he'd go see her. Then things could get back to normal.

What in the name of Shalin was happening on Kormia? What he'd heard from the Elders was the last thing he'd expected.

He shook his head. He'd been too complacent. Too eager to stay away from conflict. Had Thane been given him this duty because he'd been a death-dealer and the Brethren assumed that he'd do the deeds they needed done?

What if the Brethren learned that Thane had mismanaged the situation and there were Asazi on Earth? Brohm already had suspicions. He'd have to keep his mismanagement a secret. More lies built upon lies.

He sighed. Would he have to leave and go hunt them down now? He was tempted—very tempted—to outsource this task. He was not interested in being responsible for more deaths.

What would he tell Brohm?

He should come clean. Had anyone ever quit their position as Brethren? He'd do it, to find a way to make it work with Ali.

Ali.

He checked his phone. No messages, no texts, no missed calls. Where the hell was she?

It wasn't like her not to answer or at least call back.

A feeling rolled through him, one of unease.

19

Ali lay on the bathroom floor in a mess of her own blood. Her wing refused to be severed from her body. She's sawed and sawed. Stabbed and stabbed. She'd screamed her agony. Pleaded to relieve her of her wings.

She'd not taken into account the Asazi healing power. So as much as she'd stabbed, all she'd done was put herself in agony and spilled her own blood. The wing remained intact, but the amount of blood she'd lost had left her weak. And her wing and back were a mess of scars and lacerations. Scars upon scars, even twelve hours later.

She'd missed her shift at work. She should have called in sick. Too late now. Hopefully she could make up some story that would earn forgiveness for her no-show.

Ali sobbed into her blood-streaked hands. She threw the knife. It struck the mirror, shattering it, and then bounced back. The blade's edge struck her thigh, creating a gash that immediately began to bleed. Ali covered it with a hand. Rising shakily to her feet, she reached for a washcloth by the sink. Clapping the terrycloth fabric to her thigh, she muttered an Asazi curse.

Then she saw her reflection in the shards that remained on the wall. She was pale. The palest blue, with red streaks haphazardly covering her face and arms. Her top was a tie-dyed mess of blood.

Ali burst into tears once more. The one thing she wanted, to get rid of her wings, she couldn't even do because of her Asazi blood. Because Asazi healed.

Near Ali, her cell phone incessantly vibrated. Without looking to see who it was—because she knew, and was devastated that her Asazi roots kept them apart—she picked it up and threw it against the wall. The phone split into three pieces, the back, the front, and the battery all flying in different directions.

20

———

hane paced up and down his apartment. He dialed her again. *Come on, come on.* Straight to voicemail. He texted her, asking if she was okay. And waited. No response.

He pushed the curtains aside, flung the French doors wide. He had to go check on her. Tossing caution to the wind, he took flight, catching a nice tailwind and propelling himself toward The Other Side. He'd sneak into his office and watch, to see if she were there. Maybe she was working and her phone was merely dead or out of order.

And if she isn't there? A nagging little voice poked at his heart.

***

Ali wasn't there; she wasn't at work. A glance at the

schedule affirmed that she had been expected. There was no way this was good.

Worry pulled at him. Fear gnawed his gut. He slipped out of his corner office at The Other Side and into. He'd go up to the rooftop, hopefully unseen, then take flight for her place.

"Thane."

Thane swung around.

Brohm.

Of all the most inopportune times for the senior Brethren to appear.

"Have you contacted the Kormic Elders?" Brohm wasted no time jumping directly into the topic for which he'd traveled all this distance.

"I did. Can we go somewhere more private?"

"Your apartment?"

Thane nodded, though he'd rather the Brethren would have handled this by phone.

Twenty minutes later, Thane alit on his balcony, stepping to the side to allow Brohm room to land.

He stayed on the balcony, hoping that not going inside and getting comfortable would let Brohm know he wasn't interested in a *tête-à-tête*. Thane took out his phone, glancing to see if Ali had tried to call or text.

Nothing.

He crossed his arms over his chest. "There has

been talk of Asazi. The Elders confirmed it. It will be taken care of."

"Personally?"

Thane fought to keep from rolling his eyes. He didn't want to be guilty of lying.

He exhaled an exasperated sigh. "I'll see to it."

"Do you understand how important this is?"

All the years of keeping his silence had taken their toll. Thane couldn't do it anymore. "No. I really don't see it." He stretched his wings partially then pulled them tight against his back. "There are so many beings on Earth, what difference does one new species make?"

Brohm did a double take, as if stunned. "Maybe your assignment to Earth should be reconsidered. Saraz must be—he cannot be allowed to have what he wants." Brohm's expression was full of bitterness, as if this was personal. "You should be reassigned. You're negligent."

Shalin. No. That would mean losing Ali. There was no way they'd let him take her wherever he went next. And if they compelled him to forget his time here, would he forget her too? And even if he could take her with him, would she want to go? He swallowed a lump of fear in his throat and refrained from clenching his hands into fists. "That seems a bit drastic."

"Does it? I will seek counsel on the matter." Brohm

turned away from Thane and studied the Los Angeles city lights.

"One does have to wonder why you have such vehemence toward Saraz and his descendants." Thane focused the topic on Brohm. "It's almost as if your feelings are personal."

Thane wondered what it meant. Should he tell Brohm about the Elders' designs to take care of Saraz? Would that appease the man? Would that make Brohm back off on the idea of seeking Thane's reassignment?

"There's one more thing."

Brohm faced him. "What would that be?"

Thane released a breath he'd been holding, and with it, the frustration and eagerness to get Brohm out of there so he could go to Ali. "The Elders want to take care of Saraz."

Brohm folded his arms over his chest, his wings furling and unfurling behind him. His robes moved with the light breeze. "That would not be the worst thing that could happen."

Exactly what Thane figured. Brohm had no lost love for Saraz, though Saraz was as senior as Brohm. More senior, according to rumors Thane had heard. Brohm and Saraz had been rivals when Saraz was on Earth.

"Keep me posted." Brohm's tone had a hint of satisfaction in it. He twirled, robes flaring. His wings rose behind him, magnificent, black, gleaming. With a quick surge of energy, he rose from the balcony and headed directly upward.

Thane watched Brohm become smaller and smaller, making sure he was long gone and out of sight. He didn't want Brohm to follow him to Ali's.

Thane closed the double doors behind him and breathed in the Los Angeles evening air. With a motion as equally swift as Brohm's, Thane unfurled his wings and heaved himself upward, ready to see Ali.

ON THE LANDING in front of Ali's front door, Thane frowned. Something felt off. The lights were out, nothing shone through any of the windows as he'd flown by. There was no noise coming from her apartment. No radio, no TV.

He raked his hands through his hair and leaned against the wall by her front door. He'd wait. Wherever she was, he'd wait for her to return.

A small noise caught his attention.

He cocked his head, trying to hear better. There it was again. And it was definitely coming from inside Ali's apartment.

After one quick glance about to verify there were no witnesses in the late-night hours, Thane grabbed the handle and shouldered the door open with a fierce lunge.

He closed the door behind him. "Ali?"

No response.

"Hey." He kept his voice low. Walking through the front hallway, he glanced around the living room, the open floor plan allowing him to not pause as he briskly made his way to the back of her apartment. Still no lights on, but his supernatural vision made short work of his surveillance. With long strides, he crossed her bedroom, only to find it empty.

Turning around, he wondered if it had been his imagination. Maybe the sound he'd heard had been a cat or a dog from one of her neighbors. Though he could have sworn differently. It absolutely sounded like Ali.

He glanced at the closed bathroom door. Took a step past it, then turned back.

Maybe?

Thane put his hand on the knob, a feeling of dread washing over him, raising the hairs on the back of his neck. Turning the knob, he held his breath and hoped it wasn't locked.

Without sound or resistance the knob turned. He pushed on the lightweight door. After opening a few inches, the door was blocked. He looked down. A bare foot impeded the door's progress.

A bare foot splattered with blood.

Shalin. Shed mercy.

"Ali?" He whispered her name, half in horror, and half in a horrible anticipation of the worst. He bent to nudge her foot aside and pushed the door open more.

The floor was covered in smeared blood. She was in a pair of panties. A T-shirt was lying in her lap. Her beautiful, glorious, painted body, in her club costume, was as smeared with blood as the floor.

Fuck. What had happened here? He knelt close to her, his fingers finding the pulse on her neck. It was weaker than he'd have liked.

She moaned. Her eyes fluttered open. "Thane?" A look of confusion crossed over her face. "Where? What?"

"Shh." Where was she bleeding from? He studied her mostly nude body, still in her body paint for the club, shades of blue and green glowing beneath the blood. Her wings peeked out from behind her. He couldn't find any source for the blood that was semi-dry and congealing.

Her eyes closed once more.

He was loath to move her in case she was bleeding, but he couldn't help her if he didn't figure out what was wrong with her.

"Baby. I have to shift you to see what happened." He put a hand on her shoulder.

Her eyes remained closed. "No." The response was a whispered breath. "Please. Go away."

As if he'd abandon her now, like this. "Not a chance." He shook his head, though she couldn't see him. Using as gentle a grip as he could, he pulled her forward slowly.

"What the hell?" His uttered words caused her to flinch.

He pulled her close, wrapped his arms around her, but couldn't stop staring. His eyes refused to be torn away from the devastation he was witnessing.

Her back was a line of scars, crisscrossing and fresh. The white lines didn't seem to be older than a few weeks, yet they weren't there the last time he'd seen her back.

How could this be? Quick healing—that sort of thing was something he'd expect from a Dumarian. Not a human. Not a woman who worked in a bar serving shots.

"What happened here?" He ran fingertips over the scars, pushing her wings aside to see if the blood was coming from her back.

She jerked when his hand touched her wings, and pulled away. He held her tighter.

"Want to tell me where the blood came from?"

"No." She buried her face in his chest.

He traced circles on her shoulder, but he noticed

the closer he came to her wing, where it was attached to her skin, the tenser she became. He studied the juncture. How did it appear so seamless? He pushed the thought aside. He needed to know about the blood.

Putting his hands under her, Thane lifted her, carrying her toward the bedroom.

"Where are you taking me?" she whispered.

"I'm just going to lay you down while I check you for wounds. This blood… there's a lot of it. I can't tell where it came from. Did you cut yourself?"

"No. I'm fine. Just need some rest." Her voice was weak.

That may be all *she* needed, but Thane needed answers.

He laid her on the bed, taking care to place her on her side. "Your wings…"

Ali burst into tears, her body shaking with sobs.

Holy hell.

He pushed her hair out of her face. "Ali."

The sobs became louder. He seemed incapable of saying anything that didn't upset her. "I'm going for a washcloth to clean some of this blood off of you."

"No." Ali had stilled from the sobbing, but silent tears made their way down her face, streaking the blood trails, making tiny red rivulets that soaked her pillowcase.

She was on the bed, much like he'd left her. "Want to tell me what happened to you?"

"Nothing. I promise. I'm not bleeding." Her tone was odd, but he couldn't put his finger on it.

She stood up and turned around, as if to prove a point. "See? Nothing. Not bleeding. I need to clean up." She headed toward the restroom.

"And the blood? And the wings? I think we need to have a talk."

She shook her head. "We will." She walked into the restroom, her blood-splotched, painted body a messy, heartbreaking sight. He stood by the closed bathroom door, listening.

He heard the shower water start. Thane walked into the living room. They had a lot to talk about. Those wings. That skin. His pulse raced, adrenalin took over.

He was in love with an Asazi woman.

Wait.

No.

Ali had wings.

Asazi women did not have wings.

A sigh of relief escaped him. She was not on his list of those to kill. He could figure the rest out, as long as she wasn't one he had to kill—or have killed.

What species is she?

His phone vibrated in his pocket.

"Zale. What's up? This is a bad time."

"More bad than you know."

"What do you mean?"

"Trouble. You're in it." Zale kept his voice low, as if worried.

Thane glanced at the door. He could still hear the water. "Care to be more specific?"

"I'm flying in. You'll need help."

"I don't want you to get involved."

"They're talking about charging you with aiding the Asazi. I know that's bullshit. I'm coming." Zale ended the call.

Thane looked at the phone. *Shit.* In the background, the shower was still running. He needed her to hurry up. They needed to get out of here. Just in case.

He knocked softly. "Ali?"

No response.

"Hey." A harder knock.

Still no response.

He turned the knob and pushed the door open slightly.

Ali was crumpled on the shower floor, halfway sitting with her knees tucked under her chin and her head drooping, in a soaking heap, being pelted by the showerhead.

He jerked the glass shower door open, turned the water off.

She raised her head. Her eyes were rimmed in red. The blood had washed away completely, but her skin was still the same shimmering color that it usually was when she was at the club. Her real skin.

"You should probably go away. Forever."

What the fuck? What was she thinking? "Never. I will never go away."

"I am not right for you. I have too much baggage."

"You are not the only one with baggage."

"I doubt yours is worse than mine." She tugged on her hair.

Thane stilled her hand, covering it with his own. Her hand was so tiny compared to his. Her body so slight next to his large frame.

He pulled her against him, tightly holding her, a willing prisoner in his arms. He carried her to the bed, wrapping a towel around her, her wings were retracted, laying flat on her back.

"Will you let me stay if I show you the very worst of what I am?"

THANE STEPPED BACK, unbuttoned his dress shirt, removed it, and then pulled his T-shirt over his head. He tossed both onto the bathroom counter, on top of the shattered mirror's shards, then he pulled her to him once more, holding her close.

Against his body, Ali felt him shudder. She raised her eyes to his face. His skin took on a gray-ish black color, shimmering, glistening, scales forming that were larger than her Asazi scales. His were more defined and overlapped. His eyes became an iridescent lime green and his pupils were a vertical slit.

She held her breath. What in the world was he?

The transformation didn't stop there. A set of wings appeared, pushing outward, rising behind him. Black, thick, glossy, a hook at the top of each, in the center.

"What are you?"

He converted, turning into her dark-skinned human lover once more.

"I am Dumarian."

"I have no idea what that is."

"We are another race, from another planet. I am part of a group called the Brethren. We remain secret from humans but are here to protect them." He tilted her chin up, kept his warm finger on her flesh. "What is it that you look like?"

Ali pushed away from him, stood straight. "This is exactly what I am. She flexed her wings, furling and unfurling them. "And this is my skin. My cursed skin and my cursed wings."

"Why do you say cursed?"

"If I did not have wings, life would be different. I would not have been forced to leave my people. I could have had a normal life on Kormia."

Thane froze. "Kormia?"

"Yes, it's a planet. Where I'm from."

"You're not Kormic."

"You know about the Kormic?"

THANE STEPPED BACK. "WHAT ARE YOU?"

"I am Asazi."

"Asazi women do not have wings."

"And yet—"

A crash came from the front of the apartment. Thane looked at her, put his finger over his lips and then shook his head.

She wrapped the towel around herself tightly, holding it with a shaking hand.

Thane took long strides toward the front door.

Brohm.

"What are you doing here?" Thane hoped that Ali would stay in the bedroom while he got rid of the senior Brethren.

"I suspected as much," Brohm said, a sneer marring his features.

"Suspected what?" The icy fingers of dread gripped

Thane by the throat. The fact the Brethren knew about Ali's apartment, even if he did not know who she was —what she was.

"I suspected there was a human involved in your life. That this was why you were shirking your duties. Doing your work halfway, leaving Asazi to come to Earth. Leaving Saraz unguarded." Brohm took a step toward the living room.

Thane moved slightly to block his way, in case he should try to come closer. "And you thought the best way to handle this was by breaking a door down?"

*A*li held her breath, scared that whoever was in there would be a danger to her. Why were they talking about Asazi coming to Earth? Why were they discussing Saraz? She felt a gush of relief that he said Thane was involved with a human. So at least in that respect, she was safe.

What was Thane, really? Was he sent here to hunt her down and return her to Kormia? Was he here to fulfill Saraz's prophecy?

She tiptoed toward her closet, thankful the door was open. She morphed into her human skin, then took out a pair of jeans and a top. She slipped the clothing on as silently as she could, while still trying to listen to them.

Was Thane in danger? She had to look. Had to him Thane if he needed it.

More tiptoeing and she leaned forward, hoping they couldn't see her over the breakfast bar, that it would block her from being seen.

An inch farther and they came into view. He was the same species as Thane. He had the same dark skin, and he was partially converted to the same type of creature she'd seen on the landing, and the same one Thane had just shown her. Except this one had a cruel set to his mouth and a coldness in his eyes that spelled death.

A shiver took its toll on her body, leaving her quaking.

She'd seen Kormics, she knew Asazis, she was familiar with humans, but these creatures—Dumarians, Thane had said—they were very different.

Suddenly everything Ali knew, or thought she knew about the world, was beginning to spin on an axis. The world, this place called Earth, was far more complicated than she'd known.

Was Earth composed of far more supernatural creatures than she'd ever imagined? How was she to protect herself on this planet where she couldn't even recognize nonhumans?

She felt dizzy, listening to the two arguing about Saraz and the Kormic and Asazi. Arguing about duty and meetings.

She was losing her balance. She grabbed for the

jamb, hoping she wouldn't crash into the floor and give herself away.

She lost her grip, fell forward, her head landing on the corner edge of the door.

The last thing Ali felt was her wings pushing forward and her human skin receding.

BROHM'S GLANCE flew toward the door that led to her bedroom. "What was that?"

"Nothing." Thane stepped in his way, blocking him completely. "You need to go now."

"No." Brohm took a step closer to Thane, within reaching distance. "Move aside."

"I will not. We will talk later. Go."

"I will call a meeting. You must be held to account." Brohm reached into his pocket, pulled out a cell phone.

It was now or never. If Brohm brought anyone else here, Ali would be in danger. More danger than if she were human. Being an Asazi on Earth would spell an immediate death sentence.

Quicker than his eye could blink, Thane knocked the phone from Brohm's hand, sending it hurtling toward the wall.

A second later, one kick, one whirling motion, two

strikes with his fist, and with a ducking motion, Thane had one of the knives that was on the floor in his hand and embedded in Brohm's chest.

Gushing blood, Brohm fell onto the couch. Clutching the wooden-handled blade.

"You... will... You will pay."

"What—" Ali screamed from behind Thane.

Thane turned quickly, put his arms around her. "I'm sorry." Her eyes were glassy and a vertical bump garnished with a laceration marred the shimmering skin on her forehead. Her wings were fluttering slowly.

"Asazi!" Brohm's word was an accusation.

"Why does he hate me?" Ali asked. "What have I done to him? What have my people done to him?"

"Your *people*." Brohm spat the words out. "Your people are the result of Saraz stealing my woman!"

"What?" Thane held her tighter. "*Your* woman?"

"She was mine first." Blood trickled from the corner of his mouth. "He had no right to seduce her away from me. She was pregnant with my child when he made her his." Brohm's eyes closed. He opened them, blinking slowly.

Thane was furious. Saraz was paying the price that Brohm should be. "You? You broke the tenets? The Asazi are your blood."

Now Thane feared there was no changing Saraz's course. Whether the whole thing started because of

Brohm or not, Saraz had wreaked enough havoc and was equally guilty now. There was no way the Brethren would let him return to the fold.

"You want me to claim these bastards?" He coughed and the blood flow became worse. "I get the last laugh. The Kormic are their curse. I cursed their offspring. All Asazi will always create Kormic."

"You forced the Asazi to come to Earth. You forced Saraz to make sure they could come here." Thane shook his head in disbelief at the devastation and deception Brohm had put into place.

ALI WAS STUNNED. "THANE?" She gripped his arm for support. "My people have no idea. We have been Saraz's and Brohm's instruments. Pawns in their games." She wanted to grab the knife and drive it into the flesh of the creature dying on the floor in front of her.

His dark skin was dull in the grasp of death. "I hope you rot in whatever hell you believe in."

The creature laughed, choking on its blood, then with a loud rasping gasp, Brohm breathed his last breath and closed his eyes.

"We need to get out of here. Now," Thane said. We have a lot of talking to do."

"Where are we going?" Ali looked at Thane. They were both in their human skin. He'd told her they'd be better off walking as far as they could, and then they'd take a cab when they were well enough away. He'd said he could fly them out of there, but didn't want to attract attention in case any other Brethren were around.

Ali's head was spinning from everything that had happened. She'd thought her life was complicated when she was on Kormia. Those complications were nothing compared to what she'd stepped into here on Earth.

Thane looked at her, as if he were assessing if she were able to cope with everything. "My place."

"What about... that body... that creature?"

"I'm one of those creatures. And you are descended from one of those creatures." His voice was terse.

"I'm sorry. I—"

"You are not human, Ali, no matter how much you've tried to pretend that you are."

Ali felt as if she'd been struck physically from his rebuke.

"You don't understand." Every one of her words was punctuated with the frustration of having to hide who she was from her own people for more than a decade. "You do not know what it is like to be afraid that someone will discover who and what you are and that your whole life will be thrown into a spin cycle that is irreversible." She couldn't help it, her voice was rising.

"I'd understand more than you could possibly imagine." Thane wrapped his fingers around her arms. His hands, large against her biceps, were warm and comforting, no matter how harsh his words had seemed. He pulled her close. "Look at me."

Ali raised her eyes to his.

She didn't have to hear his apology. She could see it in his eyes, dark liquid pools with a glimmer of iridescent green in the background, announcing his saural.

"Ali, love." His lips brushed hers. "I do not know what you have gone through. But I want to know about all of it. I know it wasn't easy for you. I know none of it has been. And I want to know about the scars on your back. The scars that were not there the last time I saw you. The scars that are now healed."

Ali gulped down the nervousness that made her want to run away. She'd spent so many years being deceptive. The thought of being completely forthright was scary, though at the same time, it was liberating.

"We are a long way from any cabs, you know." She knew that the idea of getting a cab out here was unlikely to be successful.

"I know." His voice had a rumble to it that was lower than usual. Her insides vibrated to the timbre in his tone. His black eyes were turning greener with each passing second. A glowing iridescent green with vertical pupils. His human skin was morphing into large black scales that flowed down from his face, and into the collar of his shirt.

"You have a different plan for transportation?"

His wings unfurled behind him. Large and black, fanning her hair gently. "I'll take us there."

"I can fly."

"Asazi cannot fly." His words were blunt.

"That's the thing. We can't fly in our own settlements. There must be some sort of a field put up that renders our wings useless, or maybe it's a peculiarity of gravity on Kormia, but I can fly here on Earth. I suspect Finn knows it."

Thane frowned, his scaled brows drawing together in a vee, his eyes glittering dangerously. "Who is this Finn?"

Ali rose to her toes. Putting her hands behind his neck, she pulled his head down to hers. His scales rippled sensuously beneath her fingertips.

She put her lips on his, licked the seam where they formed an unyielding hard line. "He's no one. Not where you and I are concerned." Pulling his face closer, she traced his lips with her tongue, parted them, and slipped her tongue in, claiming his, letting him know that no other man—or being—could measure up or be to her what he was.

He groaned. "You are killing me. As soon as we get to my place..." His breath was warm on her face, like a blanket on a cold night.

"Yes?" she prompted him.

"You are mine." He crushed her to his hard chest.

With a quick glace to be sure they weren't being watched, he picked her up, carrying her, one arm under her knees, one on her back. And with a sudden burst of energy and air, they were windborne, flying upward at a steep angle.

Ali tucked her head under his chin and closed her eyes.

hane landed on the balcony of his penthouse apartment and loosened his hold on Ali. She raised her head from under his chin and looked around.

"This is where you live?"

He nodded and set her on her feet, but kept his fingers on the small of her back. He couldn't relinquish his touch on her.

"You're not doing too badly, are you?"

"My kind has been on Earth a long time. Long enough to build a few fortunes and own some property."

"I'll say." A low whistle escaped from her lips.

He unlocked and pushed the French door open. Waving her in, he locked the door behind them. He watched Ali run her fingers through her hair, doing the twirling thing, looping a loose curl around her fingertips.

"Here we are," she said, as if filling the empty air with words.

"Do you know how much I want you? How much I've always wanted you, from the moment I saw you? It's as if you were made for me."

Her skin turned a green color then shifted into a delicate pink. He put the backs of his fingers on her cheek, traced down to her jawline, then over her neck, stopping at that delicate spot, the hollow at the base of her throat.

He felt her pulse quickening, and it was sending surges of electricity throughout his body, ending at the base of his cock, making it swell, engorged with desire for this woman.

She sucked in a breath, her chest swelling, breasts pushing against the fabric of her shirt, her nipples hard peaks that testified she wasn't immune to him.

"Everything is out now, everything that matters." His voice was a hoarse whisper. "There are no obstacles to our being together, are there?"

He lowered his hands to the bottom of her shirt. One quick yank and it was over her head, with no resistance on her part.

Ali shook her head and reached behind her. In a deft second, the bra she'd had on was limply suspended from the crooks of her elbows. Thane pulled it off and cast it to the couch. Her skin was smooth and velvety, the blushing pink turning a more passionate color.

"Your skin... the colors..."

"My Asazi skin changes colors to match my moods. It's... I hate it."

"I love it." He palmed her breasts, cupping the rounded mounds. The tips were tight with desire, a darker rosy color than the rest of her. He lowered his head, took a stiff little peak between his lips. Sucking on it, he teased it with his tongue.

Ali shuddered, her hands rising, fingernails raking against his scalp.

He sucked harder and was rewarded with a gasp and a tug on his hair.

"No." Ali gasped again.

"No?" He raised his head a tiny bit. "No what?" He flicked her nipple with his tongue again, and again.

"No, there are no obstacles... Thane!" She raised her voice, pulling his head closer to her breast. "No obstacles at all."

"Does that mean you like this?" He could barely control his own voice as his pulse shattered throughout his body, as his cock hardened to painful steel.

He lowered one hand, slipped it inside her jeans, pushing through the fabric. He felt the heat of her before he touched her. A moist heat that emanated from her core.

Removing her hands from his head, she unfastened her pants and drew them down over her hips, leaving them at mid-thigh.

He pushed them down farther, his mouth not releasing the captive nipple. He scraped his teeth across the pebbled skin, then teased it once more with his flicking tongue.

ALI'S KNEES WERE WEAK. She'd never felt this way before. Then again, she'd never been able to completely give herself physically to a man she loved, without reservation of being discovered, without fear of having her wings unfurl.

A small cry escaped her as his fingers touched her mound, cupping her heat.

He lowered himself to his knees, spreading her legs apart. The same tongue that had tortured her nipple was licking the seam made by her nether lips.

She jumped when his tongue touched her swollen button, grabbing for whatever she could to steady herself. The only thing available was his head.

His tongue slid from beneath, pushing upward, rubbing around it in circles.

She heard Thane curse softly, then he rose to his feet, dropped his pants, swooped her in his arms, and carried her to the couch. Sitting down, he pulled her on top, straddling his cock.

She marveled at the engorged thickness with a glistening drop on the end of it.

Putting her thumb on his dew, she raised it to her mouth, tasting the salty sweetness and musk of his flavor.

Thane's eyes followed her thumb from his cock to her mouth, his breathing raspy. Sweat appeared on his brow, a groan fell from his lips.

He leaned forward, she wrapped her legs around his waist and rocked on his body, her lips parting to allow his cock to rub in the canal created, bumping her clit with every motion. She ground herself against his cock, creating shocks every time his hardness found her clit.

Thane put his hands under her ass, raised her until his mushroom head was pressed against her entrance.

He adjusted his grip until he was holding her by the hips, then with a swift thrust and a push, he impaled her on his steely rod.

She rocked while he held her down firmly,

grinding on him, sending repercussions throughout, a body that had been denied full and uninhibited access to its sensual prowess.

Dropping her hand between them, she began to rub furiously tight circles on her swollen clit while he bounced her up and down on his cock. Raising one hand from her hip, he pulled her to his lips, his tongue plundering, claiming her with the same insistence his cock claimed her pussy. A sensation flowed through her, her mind shattering into tiny fragments of pleasure while his tongue explored the depths.

Her cries muffled and captured by his mouth, the explosion grew as a choked gasp pushed her back, her body arched. Reaching for his hands, she had convulsive orgasm after convulsive orgasm, her wings fluttering and fanning them.

Thane groaned, lifting his back from the sofa, he pulled her tightly to him, his climax so strong she felt his seed shooting against her channel.

His wings unfurled, magnificent, ebony, shiny, full. They flapped and then surrounded them both.

Ali fell forward, dazed, her body shivering and experiencing aftershocks from her orgasms.

"I love you," Thane murmured, his lips on her forehead in the darkness he'd created for them, his hands caressing her back.

She raised her face and kissed his lips, tasting and smelling her own scent on him.

Inside her, his cock jerked as she kissed him.

Her body responded to the sensation. She would always respond to his sensations.

hane and Ali were lying on the couch, snuggled in the afterglow. When he raised his head, she looked into his eyes.

"What is it?" she asked him, concerned with the intent look on his face.

"I hear someone. Get dressed, wait in the bedroom." With that, he scooped her off of him and gently nudged her toward a door before handing Ali her clothes.

She waited behind the door, reminded of earlier when Thane had killed the other Dumarian. She hoped there would be no more of that, but looked around the room for a weapon, if she needed to help him.

She almost laughed at herself for that one. As tall and as muscular and formidable as Thane was, there was no reason to think she could be of assistance to him at all.

The door opened suddenly.

Ali jumped back, scared.

"Thane," she whispered. "You scared me."

"Come out, I want you to meet my best friend. Zale, this is Ali."

She studied the new arrival, who in return studied her.

"Stop sizing each other up." Thane laughed.

"She's Asazi." Zale nodded, as if that answered a question. He put a hand out. "Thane must be very taken with you. To risk so much."

Ali frowned. That wasn't exactly the friendliest of greetings. Then again, maybe she shouldn't be surprised, all things considered.

Zale looked away from her, turned toward Thane. "Brohm is missing. He told others he was coming to see you."

"He's dead." Thane breathed out a deep exhale. "He was going to hurt Ali."

"How did he die?" Zale studied Thane's face.

"I had to." Thane began to pace the room.

"You can't stay here now. If you are found, and you are together, you will be signing her death certificate."

"I'm not leaving her."

"I'm not going anywhere without him," Ali announced.

Zale ran his fingers through hair that resembled Thane's way too much. "He will be facing death, if his deeds become known."

"I am already facing death." Thane avoided looking at Ali.

"How so?" Zale asked the question that Ali wanted to.

"I was a death-dealer before. I have memories, though they are foggy. I have enemies from those days. I had to kill one already, though I don't remember my enemies. Maybe you're right. Maybe I shouldn't be in her life."

"The hell you say." Ali stomped her foot, furious at him for making unilateral decisions. "Memories? Death-dealer? Enemies?"

THANE SIGHED. It was time to let it out. "I have some of my memories of those days."

"What? That's not possible." Zale shook his head. "The compelling is not supposed to fail."

"And yet it did."

"What are you talking about?" Ali's face was a mask of confusion.

Thane summed it up for her as succinctly and as thoroughly as he could.

"So, we really have no memories of our prior lives and jobs when we are placed on Earth," Thane said.

"And you were... a death-dealer?" Ali's voice was a whisper. "A trained killer?"

Thane nodded. "And it seems as though those skills are second nature to me now, and I am able to avail myself of them as needed."

Zale was shaking his head.

He looked down, toying with a figurine on the coffee table.

"You're not safe anywhere on Earth, then. Not really. Are you?" Ali put her hand on his, stopping him from turning the little statue over and over.

"No. I do not know who my enemies are because my people stole my memories."

"We gave them the right to do that. That is the nature of being a Brethren assigned to a foreign planet," Zale said. "It keeps old prejudices and bigotry away and allows us to do our jobs fairly."

"There is still so much I don't know," Ali said. "I don't understand how the Kormic and Saraz fit into this, and how you fit with them."

Thane took a few more moments to bring her up to speed.

"Saraz broke the tenets of the Brethren when he

procreated with a human. He created the Asazi. Or so we thought."

Zale broke in. "What do you mean... or so we thought?"

"So you put us and him on Kormia? With those Kormic creatures? Kormic are our enemies. We are always in a battle with them."

"Untrue." Thane shook his head sadly. "There was no one on that planet before Saraz and the Asazi."

"Then what?" Ali said.

"First go back to the 'we thought' part," Zale said.

"Brohm confided to me before he died that the Asazi were his. That the human was his woman and Saraz stole her. And the Kormic are the result of the curse he put on the Asazi. They would create monsters."

"Brohm actually said that?" Zale looked from Thane to Ali, then back.

"As he was dying."

"Can we return to the topic at hand? Your lives?"

Thane looked at his best friend. "If we can't stay on Earth, then what?"

"Finn's cousin Kal. He can get us back to Kormia," Ali suggested.

"You will be taken by your people, who believe in Saraz's crazy prophecy," Thane said. "No. Absolutely not."

"It's better than seeing you dead," Ali said.

"I have a suggestion." Zale turned from the window. "I will open a portal for you."

"Do you know what you are suggesting? What you are risking? If they find out you helped me…"

"I know you are the best friend I've ever had." He glanced at Ali, then turned back to Thane. "The risk is mine to take."

"Throw a portal," Thane said.

"Wait a second," Ali protested. "We will end up just anywhere? Farlands? Midland?" She looked from one man to the other.

"The Elders will take care of us," Thane reassured her.

"I'm not putting my life in the hands of the Kormic."

"And putting your life in the hands of your people is much better?" Zale's sarcasm was palpable.

Thane gave him a look, then turned to Ali. "You're putting your life in *my* hands. As I would put mine in yours."

Ali nodded.

"Put the portal up on Kormia, in the Farlands. Coordinates are 46XTKCL2 by 351TK236 by 41228APKTX."

"What kind of coordinates are those? And shouldn't it be x by y? Not x by y by z?"

"How experienced are you in the skill of creating portals on other planets?" Thane smiled at her indulgently.

"Point taken. No experience in that."

"It will put us at the spot where the Elders and I meet," Thane explained.

Ali drew a deep, ragged breath.

"Don't worry." Thane took her hand. "Ready?" he asked Zale.

Zale nodded.

Ali squeezed his fingers.

24

Thane hugged Zale. "I'll see you."

"Go back to your home in Argentina. Else they'll come looking for you. I'll put a portal up there so we can visit. If I don't reach out, you do so."

Ali choked back her tears at their parting words.

Zale crossed his arms over his wide chest, his lips moving silently. A force of energy pushed at Ali, knocking her back toward the wall. Thane rushed forward, catching her before she crashed into the drywall.

"Sorry," he whispered in her ear. "I forgot that happens when others are around and not braced."

A portal opened, larger than a door, a shimmering image of energy. On the other side, through the glistening sheer curtain of light, she could see an orange, hazy horizon.

"Kormia." she pointed. "The Farlands." It was true. Thane and his kind could open up portals to Kormia.

"You could bring all my people over with these, couldn't you?"

"The people who would sacrifice you to Saraz?" Thane reminded her.

She sobered immediately. He was right. There was nothing for her with the Asazi people. She would have to find new people. But the Kormic were not the answer.

"Ready?" He took her hand and stepped forward.

"Ready."

They stepped through the portal. Ali glanced behind her at the vision, at Zale on the other side.

Thane turned around too, nodding to Zale. Zale nodded back, and the portal closed, drawing to a point.

Ali looked around. They were really back on Kormia. The orange and tan colors that prevailed in the Farlands were brilliant. In the distance, a tall mountain range spanned the entire horizon, reminding her that this area was as unyielding and as impenetrable as always. Outcropping rocks and boulders, a ground mostly barren of greenery, save an occasional stubborn and stunted weed.

Sporadic trees with a few runt-sized leaves persevered, defying the harsh environment.

She rubbed her eyes. She was surely seeing things. She had to be.

Six figures approached, rising over a hill, seemingly.

She yanked on Thane's sleeve. "Look. Oh, by the curses, it's the Kormic."

Thane took her hand, stilling her motions. "The Elders. They are my friends. Do not fret."

Ali stepped closer to Thane without taking her eyes off the approaching tall figures. They were covered from head to toe, their garments crimson and plush. When they were two yards away, they stopped, in sync, without so much as saying a word.

She tried to swallow the lump of fear in her throat, but it was persistent.

"Thane," The Elders said.

Except they didn't just speak. They spoke in her head. She wanted to ask Thane about this but couldn't. She was too afraid of drawing attention to herself.

"You had someone open a portal for you?"

"Yes, Elders. I cannot return to Earth. Not anytime soon. I have… problems there."

The Elders' faces were covered by the hoods of their cloaks. "You have brought someone with you." The timbre of their voices was otherworldly. "She is Asazi. Though she is in human form."

Ali gasped. How in the name of curses did they know this?

"Yes. She is one of the Asazi." Thane looked at Ali. "Elders, do you mind... your faces, the hoods, could you remove them?"

The Elders nodded and took hold of their hoods with long fingers, pushing them down and back, away from their faces.

Ali fought and won the battle not to gasp again, but barely. This was the first time she'd seen a Kormic up close.

The spikes on their heads were foreign, as were the other Kormic features, but that which struck her the most was their eyes. They were clouded over with a pure white substance.

"Ali," Thane began. "These are the Elders. We have been working together since I was assigned. I trust them."

The Elders nodded. "You need a place to stay, Brethren Thane?"

"I am Thane, simply Thane, no longer of the Brethren. Yes. We have had to run away from Earth. I will catch you up on what I have learned of Saraz and one of our senior Brethren, called Brohm."

"Let us go," the Elders proclaimed. They raised their hoods and turned away, beginning a trek up a rocky hill.

Thane tugged on Ali's hand. "Here we go."

They picked their way up a path strewn with rocks, careful not to trip and tumble backward. Fifteen yards up, Ali saw the opening to a large cave. She thought she saw movement within.

"Did you see that? There's something in the cave," she told Thane.

"Could be their Gostracks."

Ali had heard stories of their protective Gostrack mounts. She'd even seen a picture of them. Tall and two-legged, they resembled large birds with clunky thighs that ended with their spindly legs and clawed hooves.

She shuddered and questioned the wisdom of her decision. Either Thane felt the shudder or he sensed her apprehension, because he tightened his grip on her hand, looked at her from his spot on the path.

"Don't worry," Thane said.

"They were talking in my head," she whispered.

"That is something they can do. It eases the need to translate."

"I speak their language. The military. It's part of our training. To know the enemy's language."

He paused mid-step. "You were in the military?"

"There's so much I haven't been able to share." She looked forward to telling him about.

Her mother!

"Thane. My mother—she's still with the Asazi."

"Do you think she'd want to join us?"

Ali shrugged. That was a good question. "Maybe. I'm all she has. If we could ask her?"

"We should."

They arrived at the bottom of the hill.

Several Gostracks with half-helmets on their heads, beaks augmented with metal guards, made their way out of the cave, led by a Kormic man and—

What was that?

"Asazi!" Ali breathed out. "She is an Asazi woman." She studied the attractive redhead.

The woman walked up, her gaze focused on the Elders. Then she noticed Thane.

The redhead's face changed. Surprise set in. Then hate.

"Saraz." She spit the word out and pointed at Thane. She approached slowly. A look of confusion began to make her way across her face. "He is not Saraz," she said in Kormic. "But he looks like him. Do you know who that is?" She turned to the thickly muscled Kormic man at her side.

He put his arm around her. "Invited by the Elders. We will find out soon enough."

The Elders drew to a stop in front of the Kormic

man and the Asazi woman. "Taya. Barz. We have guests."

The redhead's face was serious. "I'm Taya. This is my mate, Barz. Welcome." She turned her crystalline green-eyed gaze onto Thane. "You. Who are you, one that looks like Saraz?"

"You know Saraz?" Thane asked.

"I was his concubine—captive. For a while."

"He is the same race as I. Nothing more," Thane assured her.

Taya turned her focus toward Ali. "You are Asazi. Why are you in human form?"

"Show her who you are." the Brethren said in Ali's mind.

"Go ahead," Thane told her. "Show her. We will not live secret lives anymore. It's okay."

Ali morphed into her Asazi skin.

"Welcome." She thrust forward and hugged Ali. Then she drew back slowly.

She'd felt Ali's wings.

"You... No... It can't be. The prophecy. It can't be true."

"It isn't." Ali reached for her hand. "It is not true. I can't explain why I am the way I am, but I have nothing to do with a prophecy. Nothing."

"But... I don't understand." Taya turned to the Elders for guidance.

"Like you, Ali will be one of us now. To be treated and revered as all Kormic are."

Taya nodded, stepped forward and hugged Ali again, careful not to touch her wings, but still hesitant.

"Let us get on our mounts. We will celebrate our guests, the newest citizens in our town."

25

Ali couldn't believe it. She was really in the Farlands. The Gostracks crested the rise of a hill, and in front of the travelers there as a settlement. Even from this distance, Ali could tell it was Kormic. A fence made of large rocks taller than two men enclosed the settlement. Around the perimeter of the rock fence, more large rocks formed another circle. In the outer circle, Gostracks roamed freely, unhitched and unchained.

Within seconds, the Gostracks spotted the travelers and stopped, sounding alarms that reminded Ali of the sound of eagles. She fought the urge to cover her ears from the volume of their cries.

She removed her hands and looked at Taya, who had a smile on her face.

"You'll get used to them. Trust me, it doesn't take

long. And they are wonderfully loyal. I'm raising one for myself. Would you like one as well?"

If she said yes, then Ali knew that would mean she would have to stay. She glanced at the Gostrack that carried her.

They'd told her it had lost its master, and now was lonely and served in any capacity it could, though it still mourned. Her heart broke at the creature's situation. She patted its long skinny neck, running her fingers over the goose-bumped, featherless skin.

The Gostrack's neck muscles rippled and a sound that resembled a purr came from beneath Ali, at the precise moment she felt a spasm flow through the Gostrack's body.

"I think you made a friend," Taya said.

Ali shrugged. Would she even be here long enough to make friends?

ALI FOLLOWED the petite redhead Asazi girl into a home to freshen up and wash her face of the Farlands red dust while Thane stood outside, talking to the Elders.

"This is for guests," Taya explained. "You and Thane can stay here as long as you want. If you're staying in this town, they'll build a home for you, like they built ours.

"I don't know where we'll be staying." Ali was relieved to have a fellow Asazi who lived amongst the Kormic. She liked the attractive redhead with the clear green eyes. She found no deception in her face and was relieved to have her around. Taya would make staying here much easier, if this was what they did.

"How did you meet Barz?" Ali took the wet cloth Taya offered her and ran it over her face. The fabric came away covered with red dust, the dirt in Kormia.

"He's Raiza's brother. He was with her and Norn, along with his brother Corzine."

Ali dropped the cloth. "Norn?" She stooped, gathering it. Could there be someone else with that name?

"Finn's father," Taya said.

"Finn's father is dead." Ali sat on a bench. "The Kormic killed him."

"I assure you he is not dead. He was betrayed by his own kind."

"No. How can that be?" Did Finn know?

"Finn was quite surprised as well, according to Marissa."

"You've talked to her?" Ali's past actions toward Finn and Marissa made her somber. She hadn't behaved as well as she could have. That seemed centuries ago.

"Yes, I had plenty of time to be with Marissa. She's very nice."

A lump settled in Ali's stomach. "I know. I figured anyone that Finn loved would be."

Taya cocked her head, quirked a brow. "You know Finn?"

"From when we were children."

"They have a son now." Taya nodded, fingering her necklace, an eye-catching piece of bone jewelry inlaid with red gems.

"That's beautiful. It's not Asazi." Ali had to change the subject, just had to.

"It's ceremonial. It signifies that I am a daughter of the Kormic now. That's where my allegiances are. How did you meet Thane?"

"On Earth. I had to... I had to leave the Asazi. What is Saraz like?"

"Fierce. Attractive, I suppose. Not to me. Not anymore. There was a time when I thought I was in love with him. I was one of his concubines, before I escaped. Both Cinia and I were." Her face turned sad.

"What is it?" Ali would have figured she'd be happy to have escaped.

"Cinia. She ran off one night. It's been months now. She's never been seen again. Gone. Lost in the forest. We tried to track her." Tears filled Taya's eyes. "I haven't given up hope." She swallowed, her throat working.

"Saraz is a thing of the past for me. He has nothing good to offer the world. Any world. Or anyone."

"I'm sorry." Ali wrapped her arms around her newfound friend.

Taya's smile was tremulous. "I am so emotional right now. I fight to keep my emotions at bay, because I don't want anyone to know."

Ali frowned. She didn't want to pry, but Taya did open the door. "To know what?"

"Barz and I are expecting." A pink color infused Taya's face and arms, shimmering and undulating, clearly embarrassment. "Barz doesn't know. Yet."

"I'm so excited for you." Ali hugged her, careful not to squeeze too hard. "I hope we are around when you have it."

"I hope so too." Taya smiled, her hand on her not-yet-showing stomach.

hane closed the door to their own private little Kormic abode. "Alone. At last." He surveyed his Asazi mate. Her skin shimmered its magnificent ever-changing colors. Her wings fluttered gently behind her.

"Finally." Her voice was so low, he wasn't sure if he read her lips or heard her.

He felt as if he'd loved her since the night he'd first laid eyes on her, but all he'd had was the tip of the iceberg called Ali. Now he had the entire glorious package of this very complicated woman.

She sat on a stone bench by the window. This primitive home, so different from the opulence he'd left behind, would suit him just fine—as long as she was there with him.

Approaching her, he held out his arms. She stood

and folded herself into his embrace. Lust made his body tighten, his cock hard.

"Mine," he whispered. His voice reverent as he appraised her face, the pure passion reflected in her eyes. "All mine."

Lips on hers, he parted her lips with a hard thrust of his tongue, plunging deep within so he could take hers captive, claim it.

A soft moan escaped Ali, shades of delicate pink and rosy red infusing her skin, merging, undulating, and signaling her growing desire. Another moan gave a sign of her total surrender and opened the flood of emotion he held under tight restraint. Liquid fire seared through his body, leaving behind a scorching, all-encompassing need to make her his, roughly, fiercely, with the ferocity of the Dumarian race he hailed from.

Her hands rose, fingernails raking his chest through the fabric of his shirt. With swift and impatient fingers, she unbuttoned it, her lips never breaking free from his.

Yanking his shirt off, she scraped his hard flesh with nails that sought purchase and pleasure. Her fingers curled around his neck before she ran them through his hair, wrapping it around her fingers, tangling in it, pulling his head back. He yielded to her aggressiveness, enjoying the passion.

She buried her face in his neck, her lips teasing, her tongue flicking, and a tiny trail of moisture left behind bore witness to her ache.

Thane groaned as her fingers slipped lower, into his pants. His breath caught, trapped, captive in his throat when her fingertips touched the tip of his painfully swollen head. Lust cinched his balls.

"Shalin," he grunted. "What you do to me." He slid his hands under her top, finding her without a bra. Her nipples were hard chips of ice against his fingertips.

He tugged on one, pulling and releasing it. She rewarded him with a moan.

Thane unfastened his pants with his other hand, leaning back against the wall while she drew him out. Unencumbered by the fabric, his cock sprang toward her, filling even more under the soft fingertips wrapped around it.

She moved her hand up and down in slow strokes. Thane fought to gain control of his faculties while her thumb smeared the drop of dew that had secreted from his cock. He used both hands to pinch and pull on her nipples, tugging them outward, rolling them between his fingers.

Her moan told him exactly what he needed to know. He could feel the trapped heat in her pants, knew the moisture it housed.

She lowered herself. His fingers were lonely for her

nipples and the creamy mounds they perched upon when she slipped to her knees in front of him. She licked the crown of his cock, then licked her lips.

The muscles in his thighs tensed, wanting to thrust. When she opened her mouth and took him into the wet, warm cavern, Thane had to grab the ledge behind him so he wouldn't lose complete control and release the very essence of him deep into her mouth.

Looking down at her, her saliva sliding down the side of his cock, her hand wrapped around his base while her mouth sucked him deeper, her cheeks hollow, he grabbed her head, gripping her hair.

"Take me. Deeper." He loved her mouth. He loved all of her but right now, her mouth was taking him to a place he hadn't ever been.

Her tongue was moving from side to side, sweeping across his girth, every sweep pushing him further. He'd have to stop her before—

ALI GROANED with regret when Thane pulled himself out of her mouth. She wanted to take him there. Curses and shadows, she wanted to see his face when she took all of his essence into her mouth and let it slide down her throat.

"My turn." Thane's voice was a tortured, hoarse whisper.

He pulled her up, sat her on the bench, helping her shed her pants quickly and spread her legs, then leaned back and stared at her, his eyes full of desire, his face a mask of lust. The way he watched her, studied her, made her want to hide, yet at the same time it created a pool of her own lust that built deep within, joined by a throbbing, insistent pulse in her clit.

"Beautiful," he hissed under his breath. Spreading her lips, he leaned in. His back expanded as he sucked in a deep breath, the muscles under the scales making a wavy, rippling pattern. He dipped his head, his tongue flicking on her folds, licking them with upward motions that led closer and closer to her pulsing clit. He tortured her with those licks, and not once did he touch that core of hers that was swollen and aching.

Ali squirmed and tried to line herself up with his tongue strategically, but every motion she made, he countered, licking with steady swipes that refused to take her over the edge.

"Thane." Her tone was somewhere between a plea and a demand.

"Mmmm hmmm?" His humming blew a warmth over her sensitive, completely licked folds, making a shiver travel over her body.

"Please." She gasped. "I need you. Now."

He continued to vary his swiping tongue with licks that didn't give her what she wanted.

Grabbing his head, she tugged his face onto her pussy, forcing him to latch on.

With a huge sucking motion, he pulled her clit deep into his mouth, his tongue flicking. She thrashed her head side to side.

Wave of pleasure after wave of pleasure rushed throughout her body, pushing her mind into a place where it shattered, exploding with the ferocity of a star's death in the bowels of a galaxy, showering her with tiny bits of light that imploded in her mind.

Her wings unfurled, but were unable to move for being trapped against the wall.

No longer sucking her in, merely poised above her moist heat, Thank flicked his tongue with impossible speed, creating orgasm after orgasm, until each was one long climax with pulses of pleasure.

She bit on her lip to keep from screaming but felt as if she were drowning in sensation.

"Help me. Thane, please help. It's too much. Help me." Was that her own frantic voice she could hear over her panting? She couldn't believe the sound of urgency and desperation.

Pulling his mouth free of her, Thane shed his own pants and pulled the bench from the wall.

Swiveling her so she straddled it, he straddled it too, facing her. Pulling Ali closer, he mounted her on his cock, impaling her deeply.

Her channel filled with his thickness, her pussy spreading to take him in, her body fighting to accommodate him while she was still rigidly tight deep inside, and still in the throes of an orgasm.

"I want to watch you come and enjoy the glory of your wings," he murmured while he pumped and pushed her up and down on his cock.

Ali squirmed and wiggled, rocking, grinding on his length, almost ready to orgasm again.

She kept her eyes glued on Thane's face, marveling in his saural features, exuberant to be able to watch his face as he climaxed, to watch his wings as they displayed magnificently while he filled her.

"Shalin, Ali. I can't—" With a tightening of his grip, he pumped her, slamming into her with such ferocity and force that she gasped.

A tremor ripped through her. She screamed as she orgasmed. He covered her mouth with his, absorbing her scream while her world spun as if she'd been sucked into a powerful tornado.

From a distance she could hear him breathing deeply, grunting. His wings flew out, blackness surrounded them, cocooned them, folding her wings within the embrace of his.

Together they peaked, his stream jetting, filling her.

He shuddered, slumped, both of them tightly encased in his wings.

ALI NUZZLED AGAINST HIS CHEST, filling her nostrils with the sexy musk scent of him—of *them*. She'd never felt so content. She'd never felt at peace like this.

She pulled away from him to look at his face.

He parted his wings and looked down at her. "What's up?"

This man—this being—this alien who talked like an American but looked like an alien. As did she, when compared to humans.

"You asked about the scars."

"Tell me." He kissed her temple, his thumb making tiny comforting patterns at the base of her wings.

"I tried to cut them off."

"Shalin!" Horror marked his face. "Why?"

"They have always ruined my life. That moment, they ruined what I thought I had with you. I thought you were human. I didn't want to be an alien. I wanted to be with you."

His exhaled breath made his body shudder. He wrapped his arms around her.

"I wish you didn't have to go through that. Any of it."

"I feel like I'm living a dream. My life's changed so much. And now you. And we're back on Kormia. A place I didn't think I'd ever return to. A place I didn't want to be."

"We're not on the Kormia you used to know. The Kormic are very different than the Asazi. You will not be forced to live a silly prophecy. You won't be one of Saraz's concubines. Saraz will be no more. As we speak, there is a party hunting him. His days are numbered. We'll wait until the fervor over their false god is gone, then we'll go find your mother."

"I'd like to have her near me."

"And so you shall. Just a little time. But for now..." Thane placed a gentle kiss on her lips. "For now, you're mine. All mine."

"All yours."

Keep reading for an excerpt from the next book in the series!

EXCERPT: FARLANDS PRODIGAL

A wickedly sexy sci-fi new adult series that continues... this time with a new couple and a new set of problems!

Qalen's the one who never should have existed. Hell, he's Saraz's worst nightmare.

But Qalen doesn't care. He does his thing, keeping a low profile, unbothered by many, living life in Midland and the Farlands. He likes his privacy.

Cinia's the concubine who shouldn't be alive. She should've been a snack for the wildlife outside the Asazi protective borders.

And she would have been, if she hadn't grabbed Qalen's attention.

Except catching Qalen's eye wasn't the best thing that could have happened. Or was it?

Enter Saraz. One pissed off, egomaniac dragon-type shifter that's not taking rejection or his life crumbling around him lightly. And he wants his concubine Cinia back.

Now.

~

Elle Thorne Newsletter

If you can't click, just put this in your browser:
http://www.ellethorne.com/news.html

PART I

1

Rodina wanted the healing herb. No, she needed it. She'd run out. Her grandmother had been one of the best healers, known around Kormia for her skills, and she'd taught Rodina the best place to get farnam, the herb that was like a panacea, curing many ailments, and healing wounds quickly.

Farnam usually grew just inside Midland, where it bordered the Farlands, not far from a large cave that served as a landmark. That location had been Rodina's grandmother's secret, and Rodina hadn't shared the secret with others. Her grandmother was long gone, but Rodina still remembered where to get the herb.

The last time she'd been here had been with her grandmother, many years ago. The supply they'd gathered had lasted a long time.

But now she was almost out, save for the miniscule amount she carried in a tiny leather pouch around her neck. She fingered the pouch which had been Rodina's grandmother's, and her grandmother's before her. The contents within had saved Rodina's life. She'd been injured once, long ago, almost killed by a slithersquil. The farnam had kept her from dying, and if she'd not had it, she wouldn't be here today.

Rodina shuddered at the thought. She still remembered, ever so vividly, how close she'd come to dying.

Rodina was in her homeland, the Farlands, but she was dangerously close to the adjacent Midland territory with its green, moist, mulchy forest floor and densely treed shadows.

She glanced back at her own lands, the Farlands. She'd never been one to venture out of her area, preferring the sparsely treed barrenness. The ground covered in rocky outgrowth, almost barren of foliage. The outgrowths ranged from a man's height to several men's height. In the distance, a tall mountain range spanned the entire horizon, making her feel safe in its openness. Yes, her heart belonged in these lands.

She looked at the dark shadows of Midland, a span away.

Too close, she warned herself. There was danger near the border.

There's danger everywhere, she countered against

her inner voice. This was true. The dangers in Midland weren't worse than the ones in the Farlands. Just different.

Midland had jungle cats, amongst others. Farlands had slithersquils, giant serpent-like beings that spat toxic needles at their prey and enemies. They lived beneath the arid Farlands. Their name alone sent shivers across Rodina's spine. At least she could see jungle cats. Slithersquils burrowed underground and traveled with a speed that defied the obstacle one would have thought the dirt created. Thank goodness the beasts primarily ate their own kind, because the Kormic—Rodina's race of people—were no match for them. It took at least a dozen Kormic to kill one slithersquil.

And yet, against her better judgement, she drew closer and closer to Midland.

A sound—an animal?— made her skin prickle.

She frowned, which made an interesting appearance on her Kormic face.

The lower halves of Kormic faces were human, except their chins had striations, raised pale lines that emanated from the bottom lip that traveled over their chins, and thinned to the point of vanishing. The patterns resembled burn scars, except they were symmetrical, vertical lines. Over their eyes, the brow ridge resembled a lizard's skin, rising to a forehead that had two vertical bony ridges merging into a skull composed of purple- and orange-tipped spikes.

She heard the noise again. She didn't recognize it. It wasn't one she'd have attributed to any Farlands creature.

Ears perked, she stood straighter and reached to the sheath on her waistband—a sheath composed of a deceptively strong webbing of fabric that housed a blade a bit smaller than a machete.

When the noise occurred the third time, she deduced it wasn't an animal making the noise, but very definitely a female.

And she sounded like she was in pain.

The healer in Rodina wouldn't allow her to walk away from another being in suffering or pain. No, it wouldn't. Not to mention, she'd taken a healer's vow: to heal, not to harm. And walking away from someone in distress was equal to harming.

She drew the weapon from its sheath and inched forward, taking small strides, realizing the commotion came from a few paces away—well into Midland.

Her senses screamed at her to rethink this or, better yet, to run away as fast as possible. The healer in her, which too often sounded like her grandmother's voice, encouraged her to go forward and do good.

And so, she did. Step by step, one foot in front of

the other, she crept closer and closer to the female making the noise.

Low moans gained in volume as she drew closer. She made the abrupt switch from the desert terrain into the shaded rainforest environment of Midland. A chill hit her, as she left the warmth—heat, really—of Farlands and entered the humid, thick air of Midland. And still, the moaning grew louder.

She's going to attract a jungle cat. If she hasn't already, by mercy of the Elders.

The cries became more frantic. Rodina rushed toward them, the urgency in the wailing concerning her. She stop short as soon as she entered a half-moon shaped clearing, the sight she beheld shocking her.

A woman, with shimmering skin that undulated in shades of orange, then fluctuated to a deep purple, leaned against a large gray boulder, half immersed in the lush foliage surrounding her. Perspiration poured down her face and neck, drenching a garment that was not only stained and torn but covered her swollen stomach. The woman—clearly not Kormic—was in labor. She clutched her stomach, her lips pursed as she released puffs of breaths with each inhale. Her eyes were closed, her hands moved, clenching the grass and dirt, pawing at it.

Rodina studied the way her flesh changed colors, the rippling of each hue fluoresced.

Asazi.

Enemy, her inner voice cautioned, this time sounding like her grandfather, who'd been a part of the Kormic army.

She needs help. This time her inner voice sounded like her grandmother.

"I can help you," Rodina said in Kormic.

The woman's eyes flew open, a vivid dark blue, almost violet. They grew wider as her pain-filled gaze locked on Rodina.

The woman screamed, and pushed back against the boulder, frantic to escape, but clearly wracked by contractions.

"I won't hurt you," Rodina told her, again speaking Kormic. She used her gentle, soothing healer's voice, one that she'd learned from her grandmother. She held her hands out. "I can help you. I'm a healer."

"Healer?" The Asazi woman repeated the word, her Kormic heavily accented.

"Yes. You speak Kormic?"

"Very little." The woman managed to get the words out between panting breaths.

"Let me help you."

"My baby is coming."

"I know. Come with me." Rodina led the woman, slowly, painfully to her home—an underground tunnel abandoned by a slithersquil a long time ago that Rodina's grandmother had added a door to and filled with furnishings provided by those she'd healed in exchange for payment.

They made it to Rodina's home, and she set the woman up on the bed.

"Ashanta," the woman said as she wriggled to get comfortable from the contractions.

"Does that mean thank you in Asazi?"

"No. It is my name. Thank you for your kindness. My people have always said Kormic people would kill you before helping you."

"My people said the same about Asazi." Rodina smiled to lessen the blow of her words. "Ashanta, do we need to get you back to your people?"

Ashanta gasped. Her skin went through the rainbow of colors again. "No. No. Please. I don't have people."

Rodina had questions, but it was clear Ashanta was not up to answering.

RODINA HAD GIVEN Ashanta herbs and tea to make the contractions less painful and, at the same time, stronger, but after hours and hours of labor, Ashanta was weak from the effort.

"One more push," Rodina encouraged her. "I can

see the head."

With a force Rodina wouldn't have believed the woman had left in her, Ashanta heaved mightily, and the baby made its way into the world, landing in Rodina's hands.

Ashanta breathed her last breath.

"It's a boy." Rodina held the baby up for Ashanta. She studied the Asazi woman. Her eyes were closed, her chest still. "No. You can't die. You have to take care of your baby."

At the same moment, she noticed the baby's chest stilled.

"No, by all that is holy. No."

Rodina worked on the baby for what seemed like an eternity, until he finally sucked air in and released a cry worthy of a warrior.

"That's it, my young, fierce fighter." He needed a name. She glanced at Ashanta, whose skin had turned a ghostly pale white, no longer glistening with all the shades of the Asazi. "Qalen, the warrior." Rodina placed a kiss on his forehead.

His wings were translucent, resembling his birth mother's, except they had tiny hooks on the tops of them. Like a talon, though soft. She fingered the hook gently.

Odd, this.

Qalen screamed. Cleansed of the trappings of

birth, he turned a brilliant orange hue, the tiny scales of his skin shimmering.

"Of course, you're hungry." She may not have had little ones of her own, but Rodina knew plenty about babies. Most healers did.

She made a pacifier of a plug of leather and swathed the baby in her softest cloak. As it would be too far a walk to go back to her grandmother's village, Rodina hastily made her way to the nearest Kormic outpost She needed a mammal's milk for him.

He squirmed in her arms.

And she needed it now.

2

At the outpost's general trading post, Rodina asked for milk. Qalen was sleeping deeply—thankfully—in her cloak, and she had his entire body and face concealed. She didn't want to answer questions about the Asazi baby.

"What are you doing with a baby," the trading post's owner asked. "We had not heard you took a mate."

Nosy witch.

"I did not take a mate. His mother passed. I am adopting him."

"The leaders of the tribe approved the adoption?" The old woman tilted her head, wrinkled, and paling with age. The once vibrant orange knobs on her head proclaiming her Kormic heritage were becoming faded with age.

"I have not sought approval. Not yet. I will, at the first opportunity. Are you going to sell me some milk or..." Rodina didn't have to say the "or" part.

She narrowed her eyes.

The old trading woman knew denying assistance to the healer nearest to her trading post would put her in a bad position if she needed healing or herbs.

"No. I am not refusing. I have some fresh cachiki milk. I can trade you for that."

Cachikis were tiny, knee-high hooved animals that roamed the Farlands, but were often domesticated for their milk and tender, tasty flesh.

"Fine. I'll take the milk you have on hand, but I'll take the cachiki, too. I need a steady supply of milk."

This was true, clearly, because she'd already decided Qalen would stay with her.

"Let me see that." The old woman snatched at the blanket, freeing it from Qalen. Her eyes grew wide as she beheld the baby. "Kill it." She picked up a large boulder and wielded it above her head.

"No!" Rodina pushed the other woman away. "Don't kill it."

"It is the descendant of evil. Just look at it. It will hate and kill our kind."

"Hate is taught. It will be one of us."

"You are wrong."

"Time will tell."

And so began the story of Qalen, born of sin and insanity, raised with love in a world that had no others that resembled him.

Rodina raised him. Loved him. Took him to the outposts and settlements to get him recognition and citizenship amongst her people.

And when he wasn't wanted by others, she stayed in her home, where they'd be harassed less, raising the baby, making him her own.

And so it was, until the day she died, when Qalen was fully a man. Mourning his adoptive mother, he gave Rodina a proper Kormic burial, packed his bag, then set off into the Farlands, heading toward Midland.

Rodina had told him his birth mother had come fleeing from somewhere in the Midland area.

And Qalen was curious.

PART II

3

*I*n the midst of the Midland rainforest jungle, dressed in clothing she'd borrowed from the camp of Midland refugees, Cinia paused. She was Asazi and a former Saraz concubine.

Was. Now I'm free.

If she wanted to call being loose in Midland without so much as a weapon free.

At least she wasn't in her sheer concubine outfit. At least she wasn't under Saraz's mind control, a sex slave without will.

Yes, but who am I?

That question remained. She'd been slated to be sacrificed and turned over to Saraz as a tribute before she'd been able to walk. From that point to puberty, and then into young womanhood, her people had treated her as a princess, though she'd been a lamb being led to the slaughter. The slaughter of her soul as she served for more than two years as one of the concubines the Asazi people sent to satiate and appease Saraz, the one they considered their god.

Only now, Cinia knew he was no god.

More like a demon.

Twisted and perverse, he'd kept the Asazi women at his beck and call, while he made diabolical plans.

Sitting on the highest branch of a tree, hoping she was safe, Cinia nibbled on the maramar fruit she'd picked. At least she wouldn't starve. For the moment. Though she'd have killed for some protein. And, no, she would not resort to eating bugs. The maramar provided her with calories and minimal hydration.

That was one of things she missed about being in Saraz's harem—the opulent food his cooks provided. She even missed the food she'd shared with the other Midland refugees at their camp.

She'd left the camp behind. The camp she'd shared with Taya, the other escaped concubine, as well as other Midland refugees. Which had included a pregnant human named Marissa and her mate, Finn, the Asazi father of her baby. Also, amongst them were Raiza and her brothers, all three Kormic—Asazi sworn enemies. With them as well were Raiza's Asazi mate and their half-Asazi, half-Kormic son.

Cinia had found herself unable to escape Saraz's

mind probing while she'd been at the camp. He'd infiltrated her thoughts and tried to glean information about the refugees. Specifically, about Marissa, who he believed was carrying his fated mate.

Cinia shuddered. Saraz. His control over the Asazi had to be broken. How could that happen? He was a scourge and should not be allowed to live. She wished him dead, daily, but knew there was no one to kill him. The Asazi would die to protect him.

Unless they find out the truth.

That would never happen.

Niptak scurried along her arm. No longer than her palm, the little furry creature she'd saved from a predatory bird's talons had recovered. He was young, umbilical cord barely detached, so she guessed he was less than two weeks when she found him.

Niptak was one of the native Midland creatures, a flyn, which was a tiny furry being with wings made of webbed flesh between their legs. Flyn glided from tree to tree, eating fruit and avoiding predators.

Niptak reached the end of her hand. She tore off a piece of the marmar fruit's flesh and held it out to him. With tiny clawed digits, he took the fruit and dug sharp teeth into it, his large luminous eyes studying Cinia while he chewed.

"Not bad, is it?" She ran her fingertip along his

head, scratching. Niptak leaned into her fingers, clearly enjoying the sensation.

Niptak tilted his head, his eyes busy studying the foliage for predators. He stilled.

"What is it, boy?" Cinia whispered, glancing about.

When Niptak began to eat again, she breathed a sigh of relief at the false alarm.

The last thing she needed was a jungle cat trying to have her for lunch.

AFTERWORD

Next in the *Ultimate Passage* Series:

Farlands Prodigal

SCI-FI ROMANCE BY ELLE THORNE

The website has the most current releases! www.ElleThorne.com

Sci-Fi Romances

Ultimate Passage Series

Her Alien Savior

His Human Hellion

Midland Refugee

Runaway Renegade

Cosmic Forces Series

Torrent

Operation Outreach Series

Wrath

Rush

Chaos

Shifters Forever Worlds

Shifter Realms

THE SHIFTERS FOREVER WORLDS

SHIFTERS FOREVER SERIES

Are you ready for it?

I have a whole world full of shifters to share with you.

I'm listing them here, in the suggested reading order, though I've tried to make it so that you can pick up anywhere in the series as we all have probably done that at one point or another.

Many of these are organized in box sets for savings. Be sure to visit www.ellethorne.com to see which box sets are out!

Where's the best place to start? Well, probably with SHIFTERS FOREVER.

SHIFTERS FOREVER

Grizzly bear shifters and their mates steam up the pages in these swoon-worthy paranormal romances. From trespassers with hidden agendas to curvaceous women who are ready to take a chance, the stories in this collection will capture your heart.

- PROTECTION
- SEDUCTION
- PERSUASION
- INVITATION
- TEMPTATION
- ATTRACTION

ALWAYS AFTER DARK

A spinoff with the white tiger from Shifters Forever: Vax, born Vittorio Tiero. He's the one that helped Kane out during a shifter battle. Follow the Tiero family, a group of white tiger shifters, as they head to America to find love... and heart-stopping danger. Full of romance, suspense, and gritty drama, this red-hot collection is sure to entertain!

- CONTROVERSY
- TERRITORY
- ADVERSARY
- SANCTUARY

NEVER AFTER DARK

Another spinoff that takes place in Europe. Here we visit cities along the Mediterranean and meet the old school Tiero white tiger shifters who are resistant to change.

- FORBIDDEN
- FORSAKEN
- FORGOTTEN
- FOREPLAY

ONLY AFTER DARK

Taking place in New Orleans, the Arceneaux shifters, led by Lézare, Vax's white tiger cousin—on his mother's side—are sure to capture your hearts. The Arceneaux are the black sheep of the family. Lézare doesn't cave to public opinion. He dictates policy in the area he rules and he shuns old school European rules and regimes.

- DESIRABLE
- INSATIABLE
- COMBUSTIBLE
- UNDENIABLE
- INEVITABLE

- Inescapable

BITTER FALLS FOREVER

This romance features Mae Forester's nephew Dane Forester, a freewheeling, sexy, successful, movie star who uses every role and every woman to escape and forget the heartbreak he left in Bitter Falls.

- Unbound

BARELY AFTER DARK

This series features more of Mae Forester's nephews! Grizzly bear shifters steam up the pages in these swoon-worthy paranormal romances. From trespassers with hidden agendas to curvaceous women who are ready to take a chance, the stories in this collection will capture your heart.

- Cross
- Lance
- Judge

Ever After Dark

Get ready to be introduced to the white tigers you learned to love in Always After Dark, Never After Dark, and Only After Dark. See their heritage. Visit Giovanni Tiero and his brothers Federico and Tito. Get reacquainted with Isabel Tiero and meet her sister Capriana Valenti.

- Stonebound
- Formidable

Shifters Forever After

This series follows a group of polar bears in New York. Russian and rumored to be mobbed up, they are a powerhouse of shifters, determining the fate of many on the East Coast. Mikhail Romanoff, Layla's father, runs this outfit with an iron fist. Layla's sexy cousin Malachi features prominently in this series.

- Complication
- Fascination
- Motivation
- Captivation
- Flirtation
- Infatuation

FOREVER AFTER DARK

A series which takes place in Denver, Colorado. Enter a world of secrets and forbidden love. Panther shifters who who share their worlds with elementals must decide who they can trust—and who they can't live without.

- NOTORIOUS
- SCANDALOUS
- DELICIOUS
- PERILOUS

SHIFTERS FOREVER MORE Grizzly bear shifters, dragon shifters, sorceresses, elementals, and all types of other paranormal beings and their mates steam up the pages as the Bear Canyon Valley clan sorts through trespassers with hidden agenda, hidden military compounds, top secret experiments and curvaceous women who are ready to take a chance. The romances in this collection will capture your heart and leave your head spinning!

- CONFUSION
- DECISION
- POSSESSION

- ILLUSION
- PASSION
- IMPRESSION

FINALLY AFTER DARK

Follow a pack of dire wolves as they encounter Valkyrie and Berserkers and determine the origins of their kind throughout the ages, while discovering their fated mates.

- ORIGINS
- CHALLENGE
- DAMAGE
- RAVAGE
- MORE TO FOLLOW!

I do hope you'll be able to join me on this wonderful journey with our Shifters Forever Worlds Shifters and their mates!

To receive exclusive updates from Elle Thorne and to be the first to get your hands on the next release, please sign up for her mailing list.

Elle Thorne Newsletter

If you can't click, just put this in your browser:
http://www.ellethorne.com/contact

My personal guarantee:

This will only be used to announce new releases and specials. And to give my wonderful special readers a little gift.

SHIFTER REALMS

SHIFTERS REALMS

I have another new world of shifters! How exciting! I can't wait to share them with you!

Be sure to visit www.ellethorne.com to see which ones are out!

Where's the best place to start? Here we go!

IRON FLATS

Wolf shifters and their mates steam up the pages in these paranormal romances. From rovers with hidden agendas to women who are ready to take a chance, to unknown the stories in this collection will capture your heart.

- Iron Flats Exile
- Iron Flats Justice
- Iron Flats Rebel
- Iron Flats Maverick

More to follow!

I do hope you'll be able to join me on this wonderful journey with our Shifters Forever Worlds Shifters and their mates!

To receive exclusive updates from Elle Thorne and to be the first to get your hands on the next release, please sign up for her mailing list.

Elle Thorne Newsletter

If you can't click, just put this in your browser: http://www.ellethorne.com/contact

My personal guarantee:

This will only be used to announce new releases and specials. And to give my wonderful special readers a little gift.

THANK YOU SO MUCH!

For sales and news, sign up for the newsletter! Thank you for purchasing and downloading my book. Words can't express what it means to me. If you enjoyed this read, please remember to take a second to leave a review. I'd love to know what your favorite parts were.

The fun isn't about to stop. Make sure you sign up for the link to the newsletter.

Hearing from you means the world to me. This would not be possible without you and your love for reading.

With much gratitude, I thank you!

ABOUT ELLE

It took Elle Thorne years to stop being a closet romantic.

Originally from Europe, she wouldn't dream of living anywhere else but Texas. Unless it was another southern—translation: warm!—state. A southern European by birth, she wants to be near the water and the Mediterranean temperatures if possible.

Where does she like to hang out? Near a lake, a beach, preferably with a latte—extra shot of espresso, please! She's inspired by the everyday men who make dreams come true. She loves a roughneck, especially one with a callous or two on his hands. A man who knows how to fix a car, please a woman, and protect what's his.

Nothing less will do.

ELLE'S NEWSLETTER

To receive exclusive updates from Elle Thorne and to be the first to get your hands on the next release, please sign up for her mailing list.
Put this in your browser:
www.ellethorne.com/contact

MY PERSONAL GUARANTEE:
THIS WILL ONLY BE USED TO ANNOUNCE NEW RELEASES AND SPECIALS. AND TO GIVE MY WONDERFUL SPECIAL READERS A LITTLE GIFT.